THE ARCANE

ANDREW S. FRENCH

NEONOIR BOOKS

Book three: Lost in America

Book four: Gone to Texas

Book five: The Final Girl

The Detective Jen Flowers series

Book one: The Hashtag Killer

Book two: Serial Killer

Book three: Night Killer

Book four: The Killer Inside Them

Northern Crime Fiction

Where The Bodies Are Buried

The Ophelia Red series

Book one: Ophelia Red

Crime Short Stories

Call Me: An Astrid Snow Short Story

Dark Snow: An Astrid Snow Short Story

Bette Davis Eyes: Detective Flowers Short Story

Go to www.andrewsfrench.com for more information.

1 COMMON PEOPLE

A silent ephemeral wind out of the northeast, full of summer heat, covered me like a blanket. A belch of northern pollution drifted across the river and settled over my head. My black eye throbbed as I struggled to find a comfortable spot on the wall. Then someone screamed across the road from me.

I'd sat for an hour, staring at the bright lights and glittering people, watching teenagers shriek and shout in between pouring booze down their necks. Then, finally, a murmuration of students flocked outside the university bar. I was supposed to be one of them, yet I hid in the shadows. I didn't want to go in, but I'd promised I would. And I never break my word.

Next to my trembling leg was a moth trapped in a web, about to be devoured by a spider. It was nature in action, an example of the science I studied. I leant down and removed the insect as a whiff of fresh pizza flowed through the air. The moth flew from my fingers towards the moonlight. To be that close to death made my head wobble, shaking loose a memory of someone buried inside my mind.

Ms Peel was the first person I ever knew who died. I was eight years old, a veteran of foster homes and orphanages since birth. She was the only adult who showed an interest in me, the one who taught me about books, music, and science.

'Religion is the retreat from reason,' she told me the day some Jehovah's Witnesses turned up at the door. She wanted me to believe in myself and not in fairy tales. The cancer which took her at thirty broke her body and my heart.

A blast of heavy rock swept from the bar and into the street. The sounds washed towards me, sonic fingers beckoning me forward as students in dazzling outfits queued to get in. All the girls had wild hairstyles and inappropriate clothes, either too tight or too small, and sometimes both.

My shoes were wet. The large puddle below me contained something I didn't like to see. The mirror is a harsh mistress, so I always hated staring into one. I avoided my reflection whenever I could and despised anything that reminded me of how I looked. I got off the wall and stamped into the middle of the puddle, watching the ripples splitting me into many parts.

The spider scuttled away as I returned to the wall. I wondered if it observed me through its many eyes and perceived me as a two-legged arachnid god. I'd given the moth its freedom, but at what cost? The spider needed to eat the moth to survive, so had I hastened its death? Hadn't I saved the moth only to condemn some other insect to that fate? I scratched at my chin and watched those a few years older than me stumbling in the street, groups of friends throwing their arms around each other before they threw up. I understood something they didn't: their joy was as fleeting and meaningless as the freedom I'd given the moth.

I jumped from the wall and headed for my moonlight. I walked up the crumbling steps and flashed my student badge at the bored-looking security guard. I strode through the door, my clothes ten years older than me, the price I paid for bargain hunting in charity shops.

The bar stank of stale alcohol, stodgy burgers, and teenage desperation. Snooping gazes followed me around the room as my otherness shone from me like cheap perfume. I ordered a Coke, the real thing and not any of that zero or light rubbish. The bartender plunked two ice cubes into a drink using his dirty fingers. I placed my hands over my glass when he tried it with me.

'Thirty per cent of ice served in bars contains bacteria, some of which is faecal matter.' He stared at me as if I spoke an alien language. 'That's crap to me and you and everyone else.' He wiped his face on his sleeve and served some poor unfortunate at the other end of the bar.

It was an example of the low standards of hygiene amongst today's student intake. The boy standing next to me was no better. So much hair covered his knuckles, I thought he was wearing gloves. It was dark inside, but he wore wraparound sunglasses. He grinned at me, an unnerving twitch of his lips more disturbing than it should have been. No wonder I was useless at meeting people. Give me an equation to solve or a science riddle to ponder instead of talking to another person any day of the week.

I headed for the first free seat. Its tatty leather frayed and coming apart, it was an unloved and unwanted item far away from the plush seats occupied by tonight's popular patrons.

A pretty girl with purple hair sat next to me and dropped the local paper on to the table.

'They haven't caught the guy yet, the serial killer.'

The drink slipped down my mouth, a chill clutching at my throat.

'How do you know the killer's a bloke?'

She leant in close. 'In my experience, the killers are always men.' I was stumped for a reply. The girl pulled back. 'I'm Akemi.' Her eyes were brighter than the disco lights dazzling above my head. 'It means the beauty of dawn.'

'I'm Alice.' I wasn't sure if I should shake her hand or not.

'I know who you are.' She had a smile like a light bulb and a laugh reminiscent of a kitten purring.

'Oh.' I struggled for more words.

'Everyone at the university knows about the sixteen-year-old girl with the piercing blue eyes. People say you're a teenage prodigy, a science whizz kid.'

I scrunched my face and squashed my lips together. 'Is that a good thing?'

She laughed again. 'I think so. Don't you?'

My cheeks grew warm, meaning it was time to change the subject.

'After six months and three murders, the coppers should have caught this killer.'

My experiences with the police were many and unsatisfactory. Their inability to understand the simplest of situations was no surprise. This many homicides in a small town shouldn't have been difficult to solve.

She glanced at the front cover. 'My parents didn't want me to come to England.' She pulled on a long strand of purple hair. 'They thought someone would murder me as soon as I got to my university digs.'

'Where are you from?'

'Pingxi. You've probably never heard of it.'

I shook my head. 'I have a comprehensive knowledge of world geography. And I know all about the Sky Lantern Festival in Pingxi. I'd love to go someday.'

Akemi laughed. 'Perhaps you will, Alice. And what wish would you write on your sky lantern?'

She threw me with the question. I'd only ever wanted one thing in life, but I'd given up on that a long time ago. I didn't know how to reply, so I checked the time on my phone. It was approaching ten o'clock, and the bar would be open for another three hours. The DJ was playing some entertaining Korean surf pop, and I tapped along to the tune without realising it and changed the subject.

'Are you worried about your parents in Taiwan?'

Her eyebrows arched towards me. 'Because of China?' I nodded. 'No, they're always huffing and puffing about the island they believe is theirs, but they'd never provoke the Americans into doing something nobody wants.' She leant in close to me. 'Do you want to know my secret, of why I'm studying at Teesside University?'

I gripped the chair as her perfume clouded my senses. 'What secret?'

Kate Bush was singing about hounds of love as Akemi whispered below the music.

'I'm here to study the techniques of plutonium production for our secret nuclear programme. The Chinese won't bother us after that.' My lack of experience in social interactions meant I couldn't tell if she was serious or not. Then she winked and laughed at me. 'Higher, further, faster.'

'What?'

'It's from the movie *Captain Marvel*. I've seen it twelve times. How about you?'

'I don't watch movies or television. They're chewing gum for the eyes.'

She grinned at me. 'So what do you do for entertainment? I'm guessing you've got no mates.'

'I have my books, my music, and my studies. That's all I need.' I rubbed at the tension in my forehead. 'I need to leave now.'

'The university warned students about walking alone at night.'

I searched for her friends. 'Your mates have left you.'

'Yours haven't arrived.'

'I'll be waiting a long time for them.'

'It looks like we walk home together then.'

'That's presumptuous of you.'

'It's just the way I'm sat.' Something strange burst from my mouth, and it took me a few seconds to realise I was laughing. Akemi put her hand on my arm. 'Perhaps we should leave. Where do you live?'

My brain was a blank sheet, forgetting where I'd been staying the last two weeks. It returned when I shook the numbskulls from my mind.

'I've got a rented flat on the far side of the park. What about you?'

We stood, and she guided me towards the exit.

'Same direction as you, but in university digs. We can keep each other company.' Akemi linked arms with me. 'What happened to your eye?'

'I dropped a tin of beans on my head.'

They'd made the cupboards in the flat for giants.

The air warmed my face as we got outside, and we headed down the first side street.

'What are you studying?'

'I'm here for biology, physics, and mathematics. Then I'll move on to medicine.' Students pushed past us, heading into the place we'd left. 'Shouldn't we aim for the main road and the street lights?' It was a longer route, but the illumination would provide a blanket of safety. The gloom we were trudging through was darker than chocolate cake.

Akemi removed her arm from mine and waved her hand in the air.

'It's much quicker this way.'

The wind turned dagger-sharp. 'Yes, you're right, plus it's freezing.'

We picked up the pace, striding by sallow looking dogs and upturned rubbish bins. I smelt fresh kebabs and fried chicken coming from the other direction.

She ran ahead of me. 'We can cut through the park.'

Before I could reply, she was across the road and climbing the fence. Then, she disappeared into the bushes. A taxi just missed me as I stepped into the road. When I reached the railing, she screamed.

'Akemi!' I shouted as I scrambled over the rusted metal. Gravity got the better of me, crashing me through the bushes and into the filth below. As I hit the ground, I rolled next to her.

'Some good you'd be in an emergency.' She spat dirt from her mouth. We helped each other up and dusted mud from our clothes.

'I tried my best.' My ribs ached and the wind messed up my hair.

'I trained as a gymnast in Taipei.' She shook her head. 'Fancy getting caught by an overhanging branch.'

We stepped out of the bushes and in front of the tennis courts. Leaves rolled across the white lines as the breeze blew us forward.

'I thought the killer might have snatched you.'

There was a thump against my heart. I'd only just met

this girl, but imagining her death hit me like a sledgehammer.

She stopped near a park bench and stared at me. 'How do you know I'm not the murderer?'

'Because you told me the killer is a bloke.'

Moonlight bathed us as she let out an enormous laugh. 'I like you, Alice. I think we'll be great friends.'

That terrified me. Having friends meant eventual disappointment, heartache and abandonment. We continued walking. Arms around each other's shoulders, we were plodding through the park when she stopped and peered at me.

'What's a sixteen-year-old doing at university?'

'My father died before I was born. Then my mother gave me away. I spent the rest of my life being passed from the orphanage to care home to foster homes. None of them stuck, but a charity called Artemis ran most of them. They discovered how clever I was on my tenth birthday, and they've financed my education ever since. I wanted to be the first woman on Mars, but I doubt we'll get a mission to the Red Planet in my lifetime. So I'm focusing on maths, biology and physics.'

'Wow.' Akemi appeared impressed.

'What about you?'

Before she replied, a long howling sound burst through the forest.

Akemi gripped my arm. 'Do they have wolves around here?'

'Wolves were exterminated from Britain centuries ago.'

I twisted my head to scan the area. There was nothing in the park apart from us and a bunch of moths nipping at the light.

Then something hairy hit me, and we went flying.

2 PARKLIFE

I hit the ground and rolled on to my side, a stabbing pain rippling through my hand. I removed the twig stuck in my palm and scowled. Where was Akemi? My ribs throbbed as I got up. Something had smashed into us, possibly a dog. I twisted my head, but didn't see any danger.

Then the sobbing started.

Akemi was slumped against a tree, half-hidden in the shadows. I ran to her, ignoring the ache in my side and the soreness in my hand. Leaves and dry mud covered her as if she'd crawled there. I bent my swollen hips and took hold of her hands.

'Are you okay?'

'What happened?' Her voice shivered as she held my fingers. Light bounced off the moon and crossed her face, highlighting a cut on her cheek and confusion in her eyes.

'Can you stand?'

I scanned the area. If it was a dog, it had to be a big one and could be nearby. I lifted her. The trees whispered, a faint rustle clutching at my ears. There was a bruise on Akemi's forehead, turning an ugly shade of purple. An aroma of freshwater drifted in. The lake must be close, but it was hard to see in the gloom. The hairs on my arms prickled upwards, straining against my clothes. The whispering continued to murmur, but it didn't come from the trees. Something was with us. Akemi's eyes bulged, her lips trembling. She felt it too.

'It's two for the price of one.'

He strode from the shadows. Akemi flinched, but I stood still. It was hairy hands from the bar. Drunken men didn't scare me, especially ones as puny as this. He was tall, but supermodel thin.

'Did you attack us?' Heat flared across my cheeks. He wore those same stupid glasses. He grinned and removed them, the hair on his fingers even thicker than before. He gazed into my face. His right eye was golden yellow gone to seed, lined with cracks as if it had split apart and was then stitched back together; the left was dark and empty.

'Will you fight? I like the feisty ones.'

'Enjoy this then.' I kicked out with the bottom of my foot. The sound of his knee cracking was vindication for me spending a year on a kickboxing course. He dropped to the floor as I pulled Akemi away.

'Come on. He won't be able to catch up on one good leg.' I tried to run, but there was lead in her feet.

Her legs moved as she spoke. 'Is he the serial killer?'

'It doesn't matter. Let's get out of here.' The boating lake was up ahead. I glanced around to make sure he didn't follow. Leaves and shattered branches surrounded us.

'You should call the police on your phone. I think I lost mine climbing over the fence.' Her lips trembled. I didn't tell her I'd left my mobile at home.

A whoosh flew over our heads. Hairy hands fell from

the sky and landed in front of me. His knee was fine, and he'd done the impossible. My heart skipped a beat.

'They were right about you; you are a brawler.' His voice was like nails dragged across glass. Akemi shook. I gripped her hand and pulled her towards our exit.

I glared at him. 'Who was right about me?' It didn't matter; I needed him distracted so Akemi could make a run for it. I didn't care how he'd managed that jump; I'd break both his knees next time. His legs were skinny; it shouldn't be that hard.

'You've made plenty of enemies, girl, but I'm the lucky one who'll collect the bounty.'

'Get ready to go,' I whispered to Akemi, hoping she'd snapped out of her shock, my gaze fixed on him. 'I've no idea what you're talking about.'

He removed his jacket and shirt, dropping them to the ground. Tattoos covered his flesh, a strange bunch of symbols reminiscent of mathematical codes and hiero-glyphics.

'Perhaps this will jog your memory.' He held out his hands, and I watched dumbfounded as the hair grew over his knuckles and his fingers, up his arms and spread across his chest until his skin resembled a fluffy carpet. It had to be a trick.

'Do you want a razor?' I'd fought larger lugs than him in my kickboxing classes. If you hit them in the sweet spot with the proper force, they'd crash to the ground.

He ignored the question as his nails increased in size until they were as long as his fingers. The hair on his face followed suit, so he looked like a constipated poodle. Finally, his teeth grew from his mouth and sprang beyond his lips. My mind buzzed, trying to work out how he created such trickery.

'I have to take you with me, but I haven't eaten all day, so your little friend will make a tasty snack.'

Those words shook Akemi from her daze, and she sprinted for the lake. I had to keep this hairy thug from her. I took a defensive stance, but he surprised me with his speed. His arm caught me across the forehead, the power knocking me into the nearest tree. My hip thumped against wet bark, the force making the branches shake, and leaves fall over my head. I dragged nature from my eyes while he chased after her.

I pushed my fingers into the grass to get up, mud sliding under my nails, and ran after him. I sprinted past withered trees and overgrown bushes. He moved as if he were a strange marionette, his limbs loping across the ground. It meant I caught up with him in no time.

But it wasn't quick enough as his right arm raked down Akemi's back and ripped through her clothes. She screamed as she fell. He licked the blood from his fingers as I launched two feet at him, catching him on his spine. We went down in a heap, with dirt, leaves and mud sticking to me.

Akemi scrambled up. Her back was scratched and she was bleeding. The glint of the moon bounced off the lake. We were close to the exit and the chance to get help.

'Run,' I shouted at her. I twisted my body to have my knees planted on his chest. His gaze burnt into me, his breath stinking of beer. My hands were on his arms, the touch of his hair making my skin crawl.

He flung me away with ease. 'You'll pay for that.'

As he rose, the bones in his back cracked as he readjusted his spine. Akemi stood at the edge of the lake, paralysed in terror. My fingers scrambled through the grass and the mud, searching for a weapon; insects crawled over me, damp bleeding into my flesh. I found a branch, pinning it to my leg as I stood. I walked to Akemi with my eyes focused on him. A part of my brain wondered if he had some rare genetic condition, excited by the opportunity to study it. Perhaps the disorder made him so aggressive.

I held the branch out, pointing the sharp end at him. 'Don't make me hurt you.'

His laugh roared across the park. 'I'll feed on your little friend and experiment with you for a bit.'

He was delusional and violent, possibly because of drugs. I'd heard rumours in the university about new chemicals on the streets.

I got between him and Akemi, the lake behind us, small boats tethered around the edge.

'Who put a bounty on me?'

'You'll find out soon enough.'

He leapt at me. I shifted my body, the branch in my hand as a defence. The wood deflected his long nails, but the force of the leap took us into the water. I splattered through it, the cold nipping my flesh. The branch slipped from my fingers as I sank into the lake.

Water flooded into my eyes and mouth. It ran down my throat as a wet mist covered my face. Instinct kicked in, memories returning of being forced down into a bathtub when I was twelve. The nails which cut into me now were sharper and longer than the ones from my past.

I fell further, yellow pinpoints peering deep into my soul. Hairy hands pushed into my chest, my legs flailing in the lake. If it's true your life flashes before your eyes at the point of death, I didn't look forward to it. Maybe I'd reach back to my birth and the mother who'd abandoned me, and I'd get to see her face at last.

Pain stabbed at every sinew. The darkness swamped

over me like a collapsing wall. Then he pulled me up and out. Air forced the water from my lungs. I spat and coughed as my spine hit the lake, and he plunged me into the water once more. I sunk again, drowning, grasping for safety and life. Hairy fingers dragged me up towards him. Fire blazed behind those eyes.

Words sputtered from my mouth. 'Why are you doing this?'

He was animalistic, teeth and nose snarling at me. 'I'm disappointed with you. With your reputation, I expected more of a challenge. I guess the tales of your exploits were all fake news.' He grinned from ear to ear with head bent towards me, spittle dripping from those large fangs and on to my face. I tried to raise my arms to grab at his throat, but his skinny frame was stronger than it looked.

I didn't notice where the knife came from, but it pierced his neck before I could blink. He gurgled as he let go of me. Blood trickled through his lips as I steadied my legs in the water. I inched backwards as he clasped at the blade. He fell forward. I moved away as the lake hit him in the face. My head spun like a dodgem car, my throat spewing out dirty liquid and tiny leaves. I climbed out and slumped towards Akemi.

'Are you okay?' Water dripped from me as I stared into her eyes, her face frozen in shock. She pointed behind me. I turned to see a figure emerging from the shadows. I was soaked and ached all over, arms and legs tense, ready to fight even though all I wanted to do was lie on the ground.

'I need to get my knife.' The girl strode past me and stepped into the lake. She pulled the blade from the floating body before getting out.

Akemi gasped, a picture of terror, appearing more afraid of our saviour than our attacker. When the moonlight crossed the girl's face, I saw why: our rescuer was my double. Apart from the chunk of flesh missing from her left ear, it was like looking in the mirror.

Cold rippled through me.

'Who are you?' we said to each other in stereo. Akemi picked herself up and ran for the trees.

'There might be more of them out there,' my doppelgänger shouted towards the scared fleeing girl.

'More of what?' Water sagged through my clothes, my fingers pushing the damp from my face to make sure I wasn't dreaming.

'Werewolves,' the doppelgänger replied. 'Monsters.'

I wiped the mud from my trousers. 'Werewolves and monsters don't exist.'

She pointed at the hairy boy in the lake. 'Then what do you call that?'

I racked my brain for the answer, struggling to think, my mind grasping at something I'd read once in a medical journal about unusual skin conditions.

'Hypertrichosis. It's an abnormal amount of hair growth over the body. Several circus sideshow performers in the 19th and early 20th centuries had it.'

'Nonsense,' she said.

I gazed at the body. Perhaps that's what this kid had, hypertrichosis. But that wouldn't explain the trick he'd played with the growing nails and teeth.

I peered at my doppelgänger. 'Who are you?'

'I'm Cassie. Who are you?'

'I'm Alice.'

We circled each other. Bats and owls cried into the night as I trod through the grass. She eyed me suspiciously, my mirror image called Cassie.

'Is there somewhere safe we can talk? Not your place; they might have tracked you there.'

My brain was full of werewolves, a dead kid, and a twin I never knew I had. I couldn't think straight.

I pointed at hairy hands' corpse.

'Why would he attack me, whatever he is, and why would anybody track me?'

Cassie strode forward. Water dripped from her face. Looking at her unnerved me.

'They're after you because I kill monsters. And you're my spitting image.'

3 ROADHOUSE BLUES

We left the park, past the boating lake and through a gap in the fence. We glanced at each other, my mind a curious mixture of things: about her, about the hairy boy, and wondering if Akemi was okay.

I led Cassie to the all-night café across the road. The place was bright and smelt of fresh paint. Apart from a couple behind the counter, we were the only ones there. The TV was on with the sound turned down, a news ticker running across the bottom about the upcoming visit of the American President to Britain. I picked the booth furthest from the door and slipped into the seat.

She grabbed the menu.

'I'm starving. Have you dined here before? Can you recommend the burger and fries? I haven't eaten all day.' She spoke as if her mouth was a machine gun.

I frowned at her. 'I don't eat meat.'

She puffed out her cheeks and narrowed her eyes.

'You might look like me, but we aren't related.'

A waitress came over before I replied. 'Wot wud yee leek, lasses?' She had a thick Geordie accent and the most extravagant eyebrows, stretching across the bottom of her forehead like caterpillars fighting. They didn't appear hygienic for a café. I asked for the strongest coffee they had while Cassie ordered her burger and fries. There were two identical pepper pots on our table, and I picked them up. There was no salt.

Two blokes entered as we waited. I twirled the pots around on the table, the dance of the condiments.

My doppelgänger peered at me. 'What happened to your eye?'

'A tin of beans attacked me. What happened to your ear?'

Cassie pressed her finger to the missing part. 'It was the worst haircut ever.' She grinned at me. 'Tell me about yourself.'

I concentrated on one of the pepper pots and ran my fingers across it, glancing up at the dark-haired girl with piercing eyes who wasn't me. The injury to her ear fascinated me.

'I don't share personal information with strangers.'

'Even with someone who saved you from a werewolf?'

An aroma of burnt meat drifted from the kitchen.

'There's no such thing as werewolves.'

I kept telling myself that. The strange hairy boy must have had a rare medical condition, and drugs could have fuelled his violence.

Cassie shook her head. 'You should believe what you see. I could tell you stories about what I've seen these last two years.'

Have you ever listened to your voice on a video or audio recording and realised how different you sound compared to the echo in your skull? That's what this was like. Cassie's hair was tied up and longer than mine, but apart from the damaged ear, hers was the face I'd always hated looking at.

I leant back into the seat, my spine struggling to adjust to the shape. Whoever had designed it must have worked in a torture chamber.

'You go first.'

'I kill monsters.' She said it with such determination, it made me forget for a second how ridiculous it sounded.

'I'm grateful you saved us, but that kid wasn't a monster. He probably had a rare medical condition and was high on drugs.'

She sighed. 'Do you want me to tell you what I do, or will you question everything I say?'

What difference did it make now? That boy was dead, and all we were doing in the café was waiting for the police to turn up. Of course, it was self-defence, but I was sure my sponsors wouldn't look upon it kindly. Would Artemis kick me out of the flat and the university? I couldn't let it happen.

'Why are you doing this?'

She scratched at her hand. 'My mother gave me up when I was a baby. After that, I was passed around from orphanage to orphanage, never settling until I ended up in my last place. The owner of the care home I was in tried to eat me when I was fourteen. He was a ghoul, and he liked the taste of human flesh. So he had me tied up and a large pan of water on the boil.'

It was a fairy tale, but it was fascinating, and I was in no rush to speak to the police.

'What did you do?'

'I got out of my ropes and stuck his hands into the pot. He was quick to spill his guts about the other monsters who stalk our world. I've spent two years tracking them, including following your werewolf from Newcastle train station. The clever ones shave their knuckles, but this one was lazy and careless. He slipped away from me when he got here, but I had his scent by then. It took time to find it again through the stink of booze and fried food, but luckily for you and that girl, I did.'

I stared at my mirror image. 'Where are your parents?'

She shrugged. 'I've no idea. How about you?'

'My father died before I was born. I don't know what happened to my mother. I never knew her.' I drank the coffee too quickly, the heat of it burning my chest. 'She exists for me through the words of others, on the cold paper of hospital records and documents from social services. In those pages of ten-and twelve-point text, sometimes Arial, more often than not Times New Roman, she's always referenced as Mother X or Patient X. For years, I viewed myself as Alice X, the daughter of X, or the lonely child of X. X was the woman who abandoned me. Every time I saw the letter in print or on a sign, another part of my heart drifted away. Then I reached a point where I had no more heart left to give. No longer was I the unwanted child of X, only Alice. The past is meaningless to me; all that matters is my future.'

I waited for her to say something, but she didn't. I'd needed to tell someone that for a while.

'They shipped me between care homes and foster families until now. A charity called Artemis set me up in my flat and got me a place at university.'

She looked surprised. 'You got a place at university at sixteen? You must be special.'

'They work with gifted orphans, finding them places to live and educational opportunities. I'm one of their best prospects.'

As I held on to the pepper pot, Cassie picked up the other one. She poured some of it on to the table.

'That's grand of them. I don't suppose they care about all the kids who aren't so gifted.' She said the word as if it was an insult.

The waitress brought Cassie's order. She was wearing gloves, those thin ones cyclists have.

'Are you cold?' I asked her as she handed Cassie a large Coke.

'I... I have a rash on my hands.' She'd lost her Geordie accent, stuttering as if her condition embarrassed her. I understood how she felt. Between the ages of six and fourteen, I had episodes of terrible psoriasis. It was on my hands, legs, and in my scalp. I hated going outside when it flared up. Staring at her, I wanted to scratch all over.

The waitress left before I could apologise. She went to the counter to speak to the guy behind it. I noticed he wore similar gloves. The two customers with their backs to us shifted nervously. They had the same gloves. It was cold, but not that much.

I sipped at my drink and whispered to Cassie, 'You said you followed that bloke from Newcastle train station. How did you know he was a werewolf?'

I couldn't believe I'd said that word. It had to be a rare medical disorder. She bit into the burger and bun, barely cooked meat bleeding out through the relish and pickles.

'At the station, the boy took his hands from his pockets, and I saw the hair across his knuckles. All werewolves have that hair condition.' Bits of burger stuck to her teeth and chin. She wiped it away and grinned.

I leant into her. 'Everyone here is wearing gloves.'

Cassie lifted the glass to her face and glanced around

the room. 'Damn! How did I miss that?' She didn't seem too bothered.

'They're werewolves?' I kept saying that stupid word. They probably believed they were. I'd spent many a night trawling through medical dictionaries and journals on strange health conditions and diseases before I left for university. Clinical lycanthropy is a rare psychiatric syndrome that involves a delusion the affected person can transform into or is a non-human animal; it is all in the mind.

'Definitely. They rarely hunt alone, preferring the safety in numbers. Here, take this.'

She handed me a blade under the table.

'Why do I need this?'

'Do you know how to use a knife?'

'Only to eat my chips.'

She pouted. 'You eat chips with your fingers. Do you use a knife and fork on a pizza as well?' I shook my head, confused as to why she was taking this situation so casually. Cassie downed half her drink and turned to the guy behind the counter. 'Hey, you with the stupid beard. You can remove those gloves because we know what you are.'

The bearded bloke nodded to the customers. One moved to the front door, the other stayed at the counter. All four of them, including the waitress, removed their gloves. Their hands were like tiny carpets.

The hirsute bloke strode towards us. He wore a stained apron and, apart from the beard, had the look of Elvis in his prime. He towered over me, stinking of chip fat and cooking grease, some of which must have been used to slick back his inky hair. He wiped something wet and red from his Jagger-like lips. He took a hip flask from his pocket and unscrewed the top. The stink of whiskey smacked me between the eyes.

He gulped a shot, his face resembling a man who'd bitten into a glass bottle.

'Well, since the pretence is over, I'd better introduce myself. My name is Dr Cornelius Chase, and you young ladies are?'

The waitress locked the door and pulled the shutters down as Cassie answered him.

'This is a small pack you have. Why did you follow me from Newcastle?' Her knife, not the one provided by the café, lay on the table in front of her. I clutched mine in my lap.

'The bounty is too high to be ignored. We were lucky to find you first.' He stared at Cassie before switching his gaze to me. 'But now there are two of you. Perhaps we'll get double the reward.'

I watched Cassie inch her fingers towards a bottle of tomato ketchup, one of those large squeezy ones it's impossible to get all the sauce from.

'Well, good luck with that. You won't find it easy to kill us.'

He laughed and put the whiskey on the table.

'We're not here to kill you. We have to take you alive. We'll have some fun with you first, but you'll be breathing when we leave.'

'What are you a doctor of?' I said.

Cassie held the bottle of ketchup and spread some over the few remaining fries on her plate.

'I'm a doctor of medicine. It's the only doctor worth being. Are you girls sisters?'

'No,' I replied. 'Are you werewolves?'

He laughed again, holding his hands out towards me so I saw the mass of hairs on them.

'What do you think, girl?'

The other three crept forward, the waitress on one side of the booth, the blokes on the other.

'There are no such things as werewolves. You probably have a combination of medical conditions: hypertrichosis and clinical lycanthropy. As a doctor, you should know this. Are the four of you related? Congenital hypertrichosis can run in the family.' He said nothing as I spoke, but I could have sworn his beard had grown over his nose since I started. 'Was the boy in the park your son?'

Those words shocked him, his head twitching to one side and the fuzz of his face bristling. He addressed the waitress.

'Where's Jack?'

'I told him to track the girl, but stay away; follow her and keep me informed.' She removed a phone from her uniform, her eyes ashen and grey. 'I missed his last text. He said he'd caught her scent heading into the park.'

Chase moved and snatched the mobile from her.

Cassie leant into me, her nose close to my neck.

'You're wearing Marc Jacobs Daisy Eau de Toilette,' she whispered.

'It was a present from my mentor at the charity. I hate this kind of stuff. I mean, what's wrong with a natural, healthy aroma? But since I was going to the bar, I thought I should try.'

Cassie sniffed at her wrist. 'It's my favourite. I put some on this morning, but I think the smog obscured it. That's why the kid caught your scent and followed you into the park.'

Chase stared at us. 'Jack should have brought you here. What happened to him?'

He stuck out his chest, arms pointing towards the floor as his nails grew impossibly long. It had to be an accelerated version of hypertrichosis, brought on by stress and illegal drug use. That would explain the changes and the boy's violent behaviour.

'I guess wolves don't like water.' Cassie grinned at him. 'Maybe you should have taught him to swim instead of stalking young girls.'

He hunched a little, his nails like scythes. 'You killed him?' He glared at Cassie. She pulled a piece of stray burger from her teeth and flicked it on to the floor.

'Actions have consequences.'

My back ached with tension, fingers hurting where I gripped the knife. I expected all four of them to attack us at any second. But instead, they gathered together in the middle of the room, heads bowed until they were a mass of tangled hair and fuzz. I glanced at the locked door. The only way out was past them.

'Where are the people who run this café?' I said as they lifted their heads.

They curved their faces towards the ceiling and, as a group, released a long, harrowing howl. The cutlery on the tables wobbled as they wailed. The sound cut into my ears and shivered my bones. They were taking this entire were-wolf thing to the extreme.

They let go of each other, and Dr Chase glared at me.

'Their hearts and livers and kidneys are inside us. This is what will happen to you too. Only we'll make it last a lot longer than it did for them. No bounty is worth the death of my youngest son.'

Cassie grasped my arm.

Then Chase and his family leapt at us in unison.

4 HAPPY HOUSE

Cassie sprayed ketchup in the air as I grabbed hold of her plate with my free hand. The sauce hit the waitress and the doctor in the eyes, distracting them as she slashed their faces. I smashed the dish into the cheekbone of the bloke closest to me. Cassie and I jumped from the booth, moving through the room as they clattered into each other in a heap.

But it wasn't enough. The fourth one had hold of my arm, pulling me towards him. I needed space to fight, but he had me against a chair, yellowing nails cutting into my jacket. Cassie was at the door, fingers fumbling at the lock, unaware of my predicament. The bloke locked his arms around me and howled as the others got to their feet. A gust of wind burst into the café.

Dr Chase wiped ketchup from his eyes. 'What a coward your sister is.'

I struggled in the brute's grip, flexing muscles that wouldn't go anywhere.

'She's not my sister.'

Cassie's dagger sailed through the air and pierced my captor's eye. He shrieked and dropped me to the floor. The waitress growled before crying out in agony as I thrust my knife into her thigh. I twisted the blade inside her flesh before pulling it out, scrambling backwards.

Chase had disappeared, and there was no sign of Cassie. The injured two rolled on the floor and screamed the walls down. I struggled to find the other one before he grabbed me, thick fingers digging into my arm as he dragged me up. He held me to his face, lifting me with ease, then tossing me across the room. My body sailed over a table, scattering plates and cutlery. I ended up against the wall, legs dangling over a chair like a shattered puppet.

The wolfman grabbed my foot and pulled me towards him.

'You killed my brother.' There was hair on the table, the floor and me. 'So I'll make you suffer.'

He burrowed his nails into my side, discovering flesh and blood, and then whipping his fingers out and across my forehead. I screamed through the agony. The pain washed through me, my fingers scrambling everywhere until I found a fork. I brought it around in one swing, reaching his neck and plunging it deep. He wailed in misery, letting go of me and grasping at the cutlery sticking out of him. I limped off the table as he slumped to the floor, nestling next to his sobbing sister.

I hobbled towards the wall for support, fingers sticking to the grease covering the faded paint job. My eyes searched the room for Chase and the other one, the one Cassie had blinded, but they were nowhere. And neither was Cassie. Something unnatural shrieked from outside, a long, violent yelp that shattered the night.

My legs moved through glue, heading towards the counter for support, and then out of the building. Cassie had to be out there with Chase, and she needed my help. My fingers trailed across plastic as hairy knuckles punched me in the gut. I fell, grasping for anything to stop me from hitting the ground. My shoulder rested on a stool as I turned to see the one-eyed man stagger in my direction.

He lurched forward as I struggled up, finding the handle of the coffee pot. As his fangs headed for my throat, I thumped the pot into his skull. The container cracked, and steaming hot coffee poured over him. Some of it danced off my leg, scorching my skin through my trousers, but most of it went deep into his mouth and swam straight into his one good eye. I staggered from the café as he screamed.

Flickering street lamps greeted me as I fell outside. The night air settled on my cheeks and sparked life into me. My side throbbed as my leg twitched.

'Cassie!' I shouted. The back of my throat ached, my voice a damaged recording done on a cheap cassette tape. There were signs of a struggle: an upturned bin, a broken chair and blood on the ground.

Shadows moved inside the café. I couldn't stay there; I had to get to my flat. But what if these people followed me? Where else could I go, the police? No. They'd let me down before.

As I considered my limited options, fingers touched my shoulder. I flinched, glad it was a hairless hand.

'Are you okay?' Cassie's cheeks puffed in and out like a balloon. Apart from her regular injured ear, there wasn't a scratch on her.

'What happened to Chase?'

She wiped dirt from her hands before pushing a stray hair into place.

'Don't worry about him; he won't bother us anymore. What about the others?'

She turned her gaze from me and towards the open door. The shadows had disappeared, and there was no more wailing.

'One bloke is blinded by knife and scolding coffee. The other has a fork in his neck. I left the woman sobbing on the floor.'

'Well done, my lookalike. I'll make a monster killer of you yet.' Police sirens wailed in the distance. 'Now we need to find somewhere safe. Is your place close by?'

'It's about twenty minutes from here if we run, back over there and up by the park until we get to the fire station at the end. There's a block of flats there.' The vibration in my legs and side told me I shouldn't be jogging anywhere. 'And I don't want to be a killer, and monsters don't exist.'

I scowled while she grinned. She grabbed my arm and pulled me across the road.

She let go of me and we ran together.

'After what you've seen, with the kid in the park and those four hairy beasts, you still won't believe in monsters?'

I couldn't see her expression as we dashed away, but it was impossible to miss the scorn in her voice. It was harder to talk and run than I expected.

'As I said in the café, they're not monsters, but people with rare genetic conditions and a delusion they're were-wolves. Everything I've seen tonight is explainable by science.'

We approached the gap in the fence. I wondered again if Akemi had got home all right.

Cassie stopped and caught hold of me.

'You say this even after you watched the hair and nails grow on them? How does your science explain that?'

It was a puzzle. 'The human body is in a constant state of regeneration, with some cells replaced quicker than others. They might have a condition as yet unknown to science.'

Spots of rain dropped around us, cold fingers clawing at my skin.

'Well, he claimed to be a doctor, so maybe he and his family are genetic experiments he created like a mad scientist.'

I pursed my lips and scratched at my chin, wondering if that was a possibility until I saw her smirk and knew she was messing with me.

'It doesn't matter now, as long as we get home safe.'

The sirens continued to wail, but the blue lights had settled over the café. A bat flew over my head and into the park, towards the dead kid called Jack. Guilt clawed at my mind. We had to do something. I couldn't just leave his body there.

Cassie peered into my eyes.

'You want to tell the police everything, don't you? You feel sorry for the thing which tried to kill you in that lake. Go on then; I won't stop you.'

She pointed towards the light and the noise. My heart had a battle with my head, and, like always, my head won. I turned away from the café and picked up speed.

'Come on. I'll take you to my flat.'

It took us ten minutes to get there, breezing past the park gates, the surrounding houses, the front of the fire station, and turning into where I lived. The block of flats was empty as I dragged myself up the steps and punched the security code into the main door. My doppelgänger followed me up two flights of stairs.

We were inside in an instant. Cassie flopped on to the

sofa and rolled her face into the cushions. Before I could ask her if she wanted anything, she was fast asleep, snoring like a newborn babe. So I left her there and went to my bedroom.

Outside my window, the lights continued to flash yellow and blue over the horizon. I slipped out of my clothes, dumped them to the floor, and climbed into bed. I was sleeping before I knew it.

———

I WAS BARELY awake when the doorbell rang. I'd forgotten I was due a morning visitor.

'Don't get that.'

I fell out of bed, panicking Cassie would answer and my caller would have to deal with identical twins when they were expecting only me. My feet struggled into trousers, shaky hands pulling the jumper over my head. There was no sign of my doppelgänger anywhere. I didn't know if that was good or not. Or maybe all of last night had been a dream.

I stumbled towards the door as the bell rang again.

When I opened it, it wasn't the person I expected.

'Alice Valentine? I'm Betty Moon from Artemis.' She shoved an identity card in my face and her foot in the door.

'I was expecting Sarah.' I didn't care who she was, more concerned Cassie would jump out at any second.

'Sarah got a new job. What happened to your head and your eye?'

Before I answered, she was writing in her notebook. I touched my head, feeling the skin where the attacker in the café had dragged his nails across it.

'New cat,' I said as I let her in. She was in her thirties,

flustered and ready to drop. It wasn't yet nine in the morning.

'I hate pets.' Betty Moon stepped into my life, peering around to find my fictitious feline.

'It's okay; I've locked Darwin in the dungeon.'

Her face turned blank, eyes wide open and glued to me. It took her a minute to work out that Darwin was the cat's name, and I was joking about the dungeon.

'Can I have a quick tour?'

Her fear of Darwin disappeared as she flashed me something designed to be a smile, but which could curdle milk. Her eyes, though sparkling blue, were mismatched; her nose was borrowed from a boxer's face. I understood why she was morose.

I nodded and took her around the flat. Artemis was paying for everything and, because of my age, deemed me a vulnerable child. This visit was all part of their Safeguarding policy. From the corridor, through the living room, and the bedroom and bathroom, I waited for Cassie to pop up and scare Betty Moon half to death. Or perhaps it would be a full death, and I'd have at least two murders on my hands in the space of twelve hours.

After a ten-minute tour, it appeared we were the only people there. I'd even searched under the bed for the "cat" to find nothing but dust bunnies and the latest issue of *Practical Biology*.

Moon wasn't happy with the avalanche of books scattered over my bedroom.

'It looks like someone blew up a library in here.'

When I grabbed a yellow-stained mug from under the sink, Betty Moon declined my offer of a cup of herbal tea. I didn't even bother to tell her about the unopened packet of

Fig biscuits I found when I moved into the flat. Moon flopped into the broken sofa and pulled out her notebook again. This time, she stared at something written there.

She squeaked in the seat and shifted her legs. 'I haven't been long with Artemis, but I thought they'd give me your records as digital files.' Her uneven eyes drifted further apart. 'Instead, I've got to use Sarah's scrawled notes.' I detected a hint of tension between the women.

Betty flicked through the pages, mouthing the words she could decipher, talking loud enough for me to know she was trawling through my journey from hospital to this point in time. She seemed perturbed by the route I'd taken.

I pre-empted her question. 'I've settled in well these two weeks, and I'm looking forward to meeting more students.'

'That's good, Alice.' She found a clean page in her notebook. 'And what about making friends?'

'Oh, yes. There's a girl called Akemi and... and....'

'Yes, Alice?'

'Another girl called Cassie.' Who's my doppelgänger, and last night we fought a bunch of people who claimed to be werewolves.

Betty Moon peered at me, and I wondered if I'd said those words aloud. She put her notebook away and got up from the sofa, brushing some dirt from her skirt and looking annoyed by the mark left behind.

'Well, I have a lot of visits to make today, and I can see you're doing fine in your new environment.'

She held out her hand before pulling it back. There was blood on my fingers, and both of us had only just noticed.

'I had a doughnut for breakfast in bed, and there's jam everywhere.'

I was lifting my hand to my face, ready to lick my

fingers to cement the deception, when Betty Moon strode towards the door and ended our encounter. The aroma of blood climbed up my nostrils and I shivered. She was outside the flat before I could say goodbye.

'I thought it best to wait until she left.'

Cassie's voice came from the shadows, followed by me staring at my mirror image. I grabbed her arm and hauled her inside.

'Where've you been?'

Cassie removed a ruby lolly from her pocket, dropped the wrapper on my floor, and thrust it into the side of her mouth. She sucked on it and talked at the same time.

'I was casing the area around this place. There's no telling what other creatures might have tracked you here.'

With those ominous words, an annoying screeching sound came from next door. To my dismay, Cassie drew out a large knife designed to lop off a head in one swipe. I restrained her before she rushed from the flat and decapitated a neighbour. I pulled her towards the window.

'Look at this.' I pushed the shabby curtains to the side and showed her what was unfurling outside. The back garden had a patch of green surrounded by burnt grass and broken stones. Clothes flapped on the line between the house and a pole at the end of the garden. Pushing each other through the billowing pairs of pants and tattered shirts were two twenty-something men competing for the worst beard in the area. 'That's Bob and Terry, ex-students, once of Newcastle and now independent pharmaceutical dispensers for the town. They'll be arguing over the washing-up.' The taller one bawled again, and Cassie thrust her hands over her ears.

'That's worse than a banshee giving birth.'

The thought made me nauseous. I stumbled to the sofa and slumped into the end seat.

'Banshees exist, and they have babies?'

'Not if I get to them first.'

Cassie joined me and ran her fingers along the blade in her hand. I used the remote to turn on the TV and searched through the news channels for any mention of what happened last night, but there was nothing, only tales of a new Royal baby, some celebrity bust-up on Twitter, and lots of clips of Prime Minister Howard shaking hands with President Cross.

'We need to talk about the park and the café,' I said.

Cassie reached into her jacket and removed her mobile. 'You have no Wi-Fi here?'

I squashed my lips and scrunched my nose. 'I can't afford the internet in the flat.'

She shook her head and flicked her fingers over her phone. 'Good job I have mobile data then. The police found the kid in the lake and two mutilated bodies in the café. They're not connecting them for now, but there's media talk of the serial killer being responsible for the café murders. We should get out of town as soon as possible.'

I jumped from the sofa, eyes narrowed and aimed at her. 'Why would I leave and go anywhere with you?'

She returned the phone to her pocket. 'One, the police will arrive here at some point, and two, we have to discover what our connection is.'

I waved my hand at her. 'There's no link between us. We look like each other, that's all.' I went into the bedroom, scooped up my phone and brought it back to her. 'I've got the internet on my phone, and I checked it when I woke up in the middle of the night. There's a one in one hundred and thirty-five chance there's a single pair of exact doppelgängers. And we aren't exact, so those numbers come down again.'

She was about to say something when someone banged on my front door.

'Police – open up,' a male voice shouted.

I dropped the phone to the floor.

5 NEIGHBOURHOOD THREAT

Cassie ran towards the window. 'Is there another way out?'

I joined her and gazed through the glass, staring down to search for the blue flashing lights and police dogs. Thankfully, I found neither.

'Only if you want to drop fifty feet to the floor.'

She scrunched up her face and appeared to ponder the idea before scanning my living room.

'Is there somewhere to hide?'

More banging rained on the door. Where we stood, with the shabby two-piece sofa, cracked coffee table, crammed bookshelves and television no bigger than a decent-sized laptop, offered little in potential concealment. The kitchen was tiny, and the bathroom even smaller. That left my bedroom, with a narrow single bed, table, lamp, and enough books scattered over the floor, you couldn't see the carpet. Cassie inched towards the door with a murderous look on her face. I grabbed her arm and dragged her into the bedroom.

'Get under the bed.'

'That's the first place they'll search.'

I kicked books out of the way so she could get underneath. 'I'll push these books up to the bed. Plus, they're probably only looking for one of us, and that's me.'

'You don't have to do this.' She bent her legs and got down. 'We can fight our way out.'

'I'm not attacking the police, not again.'

She rolled under the bed. I pushed the other side of it up against the wall, hoping they wouldn't move it. It depended on how determined they were, and by the sound of the cracks on the door, they were keen to see me. I used my feet to push the books over the space at the bottom of the bed. I pulled more volumes from the shelves and piled them up to reach the top of the sheets.

I closed the bedroom door and strode towards the entrance.

'All right, all right, I'm coming.'

I sucked in my chest, straightened my hair and placed my fingers on the key in the lock. A sharp shiver of electricity ran through my skull as I remembered my black eye and cut on my forehead. I turned the key and opened the door.

There were no boys and girls in blue there, only two excited neighbours. Bob and Terry marched into the flat without being invited.

'You took your time,' Bob said through yellowing teeth. Whatever it was he smoked, he needed to cut back on it. He had glazed eyes, a faint sheen of red staining his natural blue as he pushed past me and dropped into the sofa. Terry threw his large frame around me and hugged the life from my bones. When he let go, he grinned like a jester.

'I keep telling Bob he doesn't have a sense of humour, but he won't believe me.'

They glared at each other as exasperation dissipated from my sunken cheeks and tired eyes. My legs twitched to the right, ready to get Cassie from her bedbook prison until I thought I'd leave her there for a bit.

My neighbours were the only people I'd seen every day after moving in; they'd been nothing but kind to me since I'd arrived.

'We have a serious problem we need you to solve, Alice.'

Terry's hand was on my arm. I had a phobia of being touched, but I didn't flinch.

'Is it to do with your argument outside?'

'Yes!' Bob sprang from the sofa, unsteady on his feet like a drunken kangaroo. 'We have to save money, so I suggested cutting down on the electricity, getting rid of the clothes dryer, and hanging them in the yard to dry.' He pointed a dirty fingernail at his partner. 'But this gloomy glump thinks people will climb over the wall and steal them.' He shook his head and laughed. 'As if anyone would want his shabby Paisley shirts and Donald Duck underpants.'

'Ignore his ramblings, Alice,' Terry said. 'But we need to know, what's the perfect height to have the clothesline and the best position to catch the wind? Since you're an expert mathematician, we came to you.'

I considered their conundrum, glad of the chance to think of something so mundane.

'The ideal height for your clothesline should be as tall as you when your hands are reaching up. This way, longer laundry won't touch the ground and get dirty, and you can easily reach to hang the pieces with a ladder or a stool. Ensure it's on the east side of the garden because that's the direction the wind blows in this location. Hang thicker and wider items to the back and smaller ones on the front, so the wind moves through and dries them faster.'

They hugged me in unison, squashing me between their broad chests like cheese in a sandwich. 'You're so much better than the last bloke who lived here,' Bob said when they let go. Terry gave him a playful punch on the shoulder and me a mock bow. Their contact didn't make me recoil, though there was an unusual feeling in my chest.

'What this ignoramus means is we're eternally grateful to have Miss Alice Valentine living next door to us, and we're here for her always.'

The grin grew across my face until I couldn't stop laughing, my ribs aching with contortions. *Is this what it's like to have friends?* Maybe striving for isolation wasn't such a good thing. Bob took a non-traditional cigarette from his pocket as my mind turned to the guest under the bed in the other room. Before he could light it, he let out a prolonged rasping cough, beating on his chest and slumping into the sofa. His eyes had lost their sparkle, replaced with a sudden yellow gassiness.

'Are you okay?' I said as Terry sat next to him and took hold of his hand.

'It started a few hours ago,' Terry said. 'He's been coughing up blood. I told him to go to the doctor's, but he refused.'

Bob shook his head. 'It's just a cough. We've got a holiday to plan, and he keeps putting it off.'

Terry took the cigarette from his friend. 'How can we go to Hong Kong and Taiwan with everything that's going on out there?'

They both looked ill, but I was glad of the distraction from my own problems.

'What have I missed in the world?'

Bob was about to reply when fear consumed his face, a quaking trepidation in his throat as he spat out a nasty cough. I was reaching for my phone to call an ambulance when Terry let out a similar violent burst. He spat copious bloodied phlegm over the coffee table and looked at me. His eyes went blank while his head lolled like something from *The Exorcist*.

Both of them started shaking with convulsions. Were they epileptics? Had they taken some harmful drugs? I was dialling for an ambulance as they groaned in stereo and stopped moving. Then I dropped the phone and went to them. I'd try resuscitating them; I'd watched the training videos and practised before.

Bob was closer, so I knelt over him. His face was unmoving; nothing but darkness there. I took his hand, but it was colder than the inside of a fridge. He had no pulse, and my heart sank.

His lips trembled and a small puff of treacherous air slipped from his mouth. His eyes sprang open, expressionless empty sockets that somehow peered deep into my soul. I went to pull away, but his flesh held mine with a grip of iron. I kicked against the sofa, tearing from him, falling on to the floor.

As my fingers dug into the carpet, Bob and Terry stood, their legs shaking and arms jerking. Their faces twisted towards me, mouths gaping with the foulest smelling bile dripping from them.

They lurched in my direction. I scrambled on the floor like an addled crab, trying to get up, but finding my back stuck against the wall. Bob was a few feet away, and I had nothing to defend myself with. I clenched my fist in preparation to punch him in the groin.

The Colossal Book of Mathematics flew through the air and smacked him in the head. A first edition of *The Female Eunuch* crunched his groin while a hardback copy of *The*

Hunger Games bounced off his throat. He collapsed to the floor.

Cassie appeared and dragged me up. 'I hated reading at school, but I guess it has its uses.' A deathly looking Terry stepped over Bob and lurched forward. 'What's happening here?' She pulled me away before I replied, Terry staggering on wobbly legs and falling into the wall.

My heart thumped against my chest, ready to burst at any minute.

'I'm not sure. I think they may have taken some bad drugs.' Bob was back on his feet, moaning in unison with Terry. Cassie pointed her knife at them. 'Don't hurt them; it's not their fault.'

She dragged me towards the front door. 'We need to get out of here then.'

She had it open and was ready to pull me outside when something big and smelling like a sewer fell on top of us. We landed on the floor as a large woman with the same condition as my neighbours clawed at my throat. My breath wouldn't come, chest pushed against my ribs because of her bulk. She was slobbering over my face as I tried to push her off. Cassie thrust the end of the blade against her head, a loud crack vibrating around my flat. The woman tumbled off me and I struggled up.

'What's going on?' I said as Bob and Terry lurched forward again.

Cassie stood ready with her knife, glancing out of the door as I stared at my once friendly neighbours.

'Do you think she took some bad drugs as well?'

'I don't know.' I peered at Bob and Terry with their diseased looking eyes and rabid mouths, wondering how we could stop them. The frantic noises coming from them appeared to be getting louder and echoing around the flat, until I realised they were behind me. I glanced over to see Cassie staring through the open door.

'And what about this lot?'

I did my best crab impersonation again, moving towards her and looking outside. Whatever illness had overtaken Bob, Terry, and the big woman had possessed about a dozen people coming up the stairs.

'It has to be a viral infection.' My brain considered many scenarios, from accidental spillage to a terrorist attack. Cassie arched her head upwards.

'Do these stairs go all the way up and out of the building?'

I didn't know because I'd never been up them. 'I think so.'

She grabbed my hand and dragged me up the concrete as Bob's gnarled fingers missed my arm. I had one last look at my neighbour as we bundled ourselves upstairs. What disease could have done that to him so quickly? The flesh-eating virus necrotising fasciitis can develop over hours, so if it infected them this morning, it could have reached this stage by now. But how did these people get infected? They couldn't all have taken the same drugs.

Our feet pounded up the stairs. My side and legs ached from last night, and my head throbbed. To think twenty-four hours ago, I'd shouted at a tin of beans for inflicting a black eye on me.

'They won't stay down there for long,' Cassie said.

The cold air shocked my throat and lungs to inhale more quickly and deeply. With each stair, pain shot through my leg and joined the agony in my side. There was an exit ahead, which I hoped went to the roof. Cassie grabbed the handle and pulled it.

It didn't budge.

'Bastard.' She removed her knife and scraped at the gap in the door. The wood was ancient and full of cracks, littered with stains and graffiti. If it was old enough, she could prise it open.

'They might not follow us here,' I said, more in desperation than reality.

'Don't bet on it.' She nodded down. Shadows crawled and groaned towards us.

'Then we're screwed.' My shoulder arched at the metal railing at my side, my hand searching inside my clothes for a weapon. We'd left in such a rush, I didn't even have my phone.

Splinters of wood jumped over my head from the door.

'I might get it open if we have enough time.'

The shadows were turning into lumps of mangled flesh and poisoned eyes. Bob crawled up the steps towards us, the others not far behind.

I pushed the pain from my legs and stood. 'Time's running out, but I'll make more for you.'

Cassie's hand was on my arm before I could head down. 'You take over here, and I'll do it. I've got the training and experience.'

I turned and looked at her. 'Do you have twelve months experience of kickboxing with some of the toughest and ugliest blokes in the country?'

Her eyes shivered in surprise. 'No, I haven't.'

'You're better with a knife than me, so keep hacking at the door, and I'll be right back.'

Before she protested, I moved down the first steps. Bob was a few feet from me, with his body hunched into an impossible shape. The virus had distorted his face into a mess of Picasso proportions. Half of his nose had slipped into the mouth, so he appeared to be eating it. His eyes had melted into one giant orb resembling a cyclops. I didn't know if it would make it easier for him to see me or harder. When he parted his lips, there was a gaping black hole since all his teeth had disappeared.

I steadied my back foot, waiting for him to get closer and within my reach as behind him, the mass drew nearer. If the virus had devoured his face, I assumed the same would happen to his body. Bob tried to lurch forward, but I moved first, thrusting my right leg out and kicking at his knee: it shattered in one go, his useless form falling backwards and tumbling down the stairs, taking a few of the others with him.

My heart went with them as I turned to stare at Cassie.

'How much longer?'

She hacked away at the door. 'Two minutes.'

Something grabbed my leg; a face crapped out of Hell glared at me as it slithered up. I thrust down and punched the face so hard, the whole of my fist vanished into its skull. I pulled it out and kicked. Flesh and blood and bones stuck to my fingers, the stink of the dead nearly making me vomit. I wiped away the gloop on my trousers and inched a few steps back. A gust of wind smacked into my head.

'Get up here, Alice.'

I was turning to run upstairs when something large descended on me.

6 RUN FOR HOME

The remains of the woman crawled up my legs and over my chest, her faceless head, shrunken torso, and withered hands clawing at me. Then, as sharp fingers grasped for my eyes, she melted away like the Wicked Witch of the West.

Cassie took my hand and dragged me up. We didn't stop moving, stumbling through the door and on to the roof. She closed it behind us. A wisp of wind brushed against me, my hand reaching up to block out the harsh glare of the morning sun. An aroma of death was everywhere.

She moved around the edge of the building, and then came back to me.

'There are some emergency stairs down the side. We'll use them to get away and head to Lindisfarne.'

I arched my eyebrows at her. There was silence beyond the door. Had all the infected melted?

'Why should I go to the Holy Island?'

She pawed at her chin, shaking bits of wood from her hair.

'For the last six months, I've been hearing rumours of a group of people on the island who are experts on the supernatural. If they exist, they might tell us what this is all about.' She pointed towards the door and the river of slime running under it.

I stood and flexed my throbbing arms and legs.

'This is nothing to do with the supernatural: the supernatural isn't real. A virus infected those poor people.'

'You're deluding yourself, lookalike.'

'It doesn't matter what it is; I've got classes to go to.'

Cassie shook her head. 'You can't stay here, Alice. How will you explain this to the police?'

More liquid swam on to the roof. What was once human flesh and bone slithered towards us. I moved from it and near to the edge of the building.

'We were attacked. It was self-defence. An infection drove them crazy.'

Cassie kept on shaking her head. 'A pack of werewolves last night and now these zombies, and yet you still don't believe what's in front of your eyes. Somebody sent these creatures after you. They won't stop coming.'

'I've told you, there are perfectly scientific explanations for these things. This only happened because someone thinks I'm you.' The cut on the top of my head throbbed. 'This is your fault.'

'How did science cause all this mayhem? Do you think there was an outbreak from a lab nearby, or maybe it's a calculated attack?'

She seemed as dubious about either of those prospects as I was of her continuous assertion it was all to do with the supernatural.

'Where do zombies come from in your world?' My tone

was serious, respect for her views written across my face. I'd once met a grown man who believed in unicorns, but I didn't ridicule him. Everyone is entitled to their beliefs, no matter how silly I think they are.

She stretched her shoulders and flexed her fingers, probably releasing the stress.

'When did you notice the change in your neighbours?'

I remembered them coming into the flat and pretending to be mad with each other.

'They both looked pale, but that wasn't a surprise; they always kept unusual hours. After about ten minutes, they started coughing and collapsed on to the sofa. Then everything went crazy.'

'They could have been bitten this morning, but you would have seen more gradual changes in them, and that wouldn't explain what happened to the others. It's more likely it was a spell put on the block of flats.'

I laughed. 'A spell, seriously? You're saying magic exists in your world?'

Her eyes shrank into pinpricks, peering at me as if this was all a waste of her valuable time.

'It's your world too, and magic exists, but not that Harry Potter stuff. There are no secret schools or invisible train stations; only people who crave power and others who like to cause misery and pain.'

'So, you think someone cast a zombie spell over my block of flats to get to me. None of this makes any sense.'

Cassie ignored the tremor in my voice and looked over the edge. 'Sirens are coming this way. We need to leave now, unless you want to explain your uninvited guests to the police.' She strode to the bit where the stairs must have been.

This was my chance to put this madness behind me. 'They attacked me. I'm innocent. Why wouldn't the police believe me?' Cassie stood at the edge, her eyes looking straight into me. At that moment, I knew if we separated, I'd never see her again.

'Someone killed these people because of you.' Her voice was calm, her gaze cold and calculating. 'You can stay here and wait for it to happen again and watch more innocents die, or you can come with me, and we'll find who is behind this and avenge those people.'

I turned from Cassie and stared at the liquid which was once my neighbours. I didn't believe her nonsense about the supernatural; science could explain everything in nature. It was a virus that caused this; somebody poisoned them, but I owed it to Bob and Terry to discover who had done this, and why.

The gooey fluid reached my shoes. I moved from it and walked towards her.

Cassie climbed over the side and down the ladder. I followed her, my fingers chilled by the rusty metal and face cooled by a gust of wind swirling around the building. It took a minute to reach the bottom. As my feet touched the ground, I expected more diseased individuals to rush at us, but it was deserted.

The wail of the sirens grew closer as my doppelgänger stared at me.

'Do you have any money?'

We headed from the block of flats. 'Artemis provides me with a monthly allowance to cover my food and pay my rent and bills.'

We rounded the corner and headed to the park where Cassie had killed the hairy boy.

'When we get somewhere safer, you must tell me why

these Artemis people are keen to shower so many resources at you. It can't be because you're so gifted.'

There was resentment in her voice, and anger which hadn't been there before. I said nothing, flicking bits of liquid from my hands. The smell was pungent.

We crossed the road and headed into town. Three police cars sped past in the other direction. There was no need to guess where they were going.

'We could get the train to Newcastle and make our way from there.' I searched through my pockets for money. I counted it as we walked: a few coins and two twenty-pound notes. It wouldn't last long, and I already felt like a fugitive.

Cassie pulled on my arm. 'There's no need for that. I've got a better idea.'

She dragged me into a side street full of overflowing bins and stray cats. My stink was worse than theirs and scared the felines away. Cassie nodded at the motorbike someone had left the keys in. Even two helmets were resting on it.

'I can't ride a bike, and I'm not a thief.'

'I can, and you're a killer.'

She picked up a helmet and handed it to me. The flashing lights got closer. This was my last chance to return to the flat and explain everything to the authorities. I had the university to think of, classes to attend. I owed Artemis to do it.

And then I thought of Bob and Terry and how they should be stringing out clothes to dry in the yard right about now. I remembered Terry's touch on my arm, the smile on his face, and their dreams of an exotic holiday.

Cassie sat on the bike. I got on behind her.

'Make yourself comfortable,' she said as we put the

helmets on. Mine was a little too big, but that was better than too small.

'Do you know how to get to Lindisfarne Island?' I'd been once as a kid on a trip out from the care home, but couldn't remember much about it.

Cassie delved into her pocket and removed her phone, then handed it to me.

'Turn on the GPS and search.'

I typed in the details as she switched on the engine.

'It's about an hour and three quarters from here.'

'Hold on tight.' She pulled out of the street as I held on to her with both arms, holding the mobile so she could see the directions.

It was an uneventful journey, even though I was waiting for police cars to chase us at any minute. We headed past Hartlepool and Sunderland, catching glimpses of the coast and the sea on our right.

I closed my eyes and let my mind drift away, but nothing could extinguish the images of what had happened at the flats. It was a challenge, but I relished challenges; all I had to do was approach it as an equation to solve.

A combination of genetic and psychiatric disorders triggered the events in the park and the café. A virus caused the disturbance with my neighbours. Was it all connected? The only links were Cassie, my doppelgänger, and me. It was long odds to bump into someone who looked like you, but it wasn't impossible. The chance to win the National Lottery jackpot was astronomical, but people still did it, so the actions involving me were possible.

Cassie would slow down to look at the map every few miles, but it was a straightforward route. She drove as fast as possible, weaving in and out of the occasional traffic as if we were in some Hollywood movie. To take my mind off the danger, I tried to recall my only trip to the Holy Island of Lindisfarne.

The care home I lived in had links to one of the local churches, and it was their idea to visit the place. I don't think any of the other children cared about the island's religious history; it was a day out, and that was the only thing that mattered. The adults dragged most of the kids off to the Priory, but I remembered sneaking away and wandering down to the sea. Staring at the ocean made me feel less alone in the world. But that was before I stopped caring about such things.

My last memory of it was the teachers panicking because they thought we'd missed our slot to leave across the causeway, so the tide would be in, and we'd have to spend the night there. I wasn't fussed. It couldn't have been any worse than staying in the care home, and I might get the chance to sleep outside under the stars. But one of the bravest adults powered through the oncoming sea while the kids cheered about being in a submarine.

I wondered if Cassie knew about the causeway and had checked the times of the tides. As we turned off the road, I gazed at the Priory rising out of the hill ahead. She pulled into the large car park as I stared at the water on either side of us in the distance. She stopped next to a battered-looking red and yellow mini-van.

I got off the bike and removed the helmet.

'Stick a fiver in the parking machine,' Cassie said. 'That should cover the whole day.'

'We'll be here that long?'

'However long it takes.' The helmet had dislodged a stray hair from Cassie's face. She brushed it out of the way. 'Have you been here before?'

'Once, with the foster home.' It was the only trip I went on before leaving for university. 'What about you?'

She kicked dust from her shoe. 'Nope. Until my life changed forever, I spent most of it in my room playing computer games.'

'What about your friends?'

Cassie grinned at me. 'What are those?'

'You didn't have any friends?'

'On the contrary, my lookalike. I was the most popular person wherever I went. Both boys and girls swarmed around me.'

'So how come you had no mates?'

'Because I didn't want any.' She gazed at me. 'Tell me something about you which no one else knows.'

I pondered her question, wondering where to start. 'Last year, I snuck out of the foster home and went on an Extinction Rebellion protest.'

She grinned and nodded. 'That's cool. I like a bit of rebellion. Are you allergic to anything?'

'Only jazz music.'

Cassie put a hand on her ribs and laughed. 'I know how you feel.'

'Do you have any secrets?'

Her laughter disappeared as quickly as it came. She scrunched her eyebrows at me.

'I enjoy shoplifting, especially clothes. I kiss both boys and girls. I'm addicted to crappy reality TV shows. I once threw up in someone's hooded top. Now you tell me your deepest, darkest secret.'

'I love Marmite.'

Her shoulders shook as she grimaced. 'That's monstrous.'

'Speaking of which, where do we find who we're looking for?'

'We look wherever the religion is. Priests, nuns, monks; they understand the things ordinary people don't.'

'Is this a good versus evil, Heaven and Hell thing?' As an atheist, I found it hard to believe.

'I know nothing about that. I've killed monsters that called themselves demons, but, as with all these creatures, I don't know where they came from. That's why I was on my way here when I was distracted in Newcastle.'

'Which led you to me?'

She didn't take the bait, watching me as I went to the ticket machine. Spread out on either side of me were rows of vehicles. I reached into my pocket; I had the money, but not the right change. I walked away from the contraption. What did it matter if we were fined? All the melted flesh in my building and the dead boy in the park were enough to get me into trouble.

'Did you do it?'

I shrugged when I returned to her. 'Who are we looking for on the island?'

She seemed unconcerned with my lack of a ticket. 'The Moles of Lindisfarne, that's what the whispers call them.'

'That implies they're underground.'

'So let's see if we can find any caves or similar places. We'll head over to the ruins of the Priory with the other visitors.'

We set off as the sun baked overhead, the blue of the sky looking like an azure sea shimmering above me. I hadn't visited the ruin the only time I was there, but I knew it was the most popular attraction on the island. I strode next to Cassie and pushed through the tourists, the two of us receiving the occasional strange look as if they'd never seen people who looked the same before.

'I watched a documentary once about identical triplets separated at birth as part of some scientific experiment,' Cassie said. 'We could be sisters.'

'We're not related.' I was happy to be on my own, yet still, I was walking with her to this island on some strange unknown quest.

'I know we aren't; your mind is far too closed to be related to me. What I meant was that science has done plenty of horrible things to this planet and what lives on it, so why are you so determined to use it as your Holy Bible?'

'Don't blame the science; blame those who misuse it.'

Heat trickled through my cheeks, a rare scent of anger seeping into my brain. People had picked on me all my life for liking maths and science, and I'd ignored it or laughed it off. So why was her attitude bothering me now?

She pulled me from the crowd and past the edge of the ruins.

'I've been doing some digging online.' We were on our own now, people and ruins behind us, the sea in front. She had her phone in her hands, but there couldn't be much battery left in it. 'A few years ago, archaeological excavations took place on the spot called The Heugh.'

'That sounds fascinating,' I said with heavy sarcasm. Nobody ever got my sarcasm, no matter how hard I tried.

'They found the layout of an early Anglo-Saxon church on the high ground, but they stopped when they got to a spot known as the Lantern Chapel.'

I'd lost interest in what she was saying, wondering what was happening back at my flat, my gaze drifting over the water. Would Artemis look for me?

'And this is interesting because...?'

She grabbed my arm and dragged me further away from the noise behind us. I was too tired to protest, happy for her to lead me on this fruitless quest to find things that didn't exist.

'It's interesting because, instead of carrying on, they stopped with no explanation. Perhaps they were warned off because there's something under that part of the ground.'

Her voice rose a pitch and there was a glint in her eyes. Did I look like that when I was excited? I tried to remember the last time I was excited; it was when Artemis told me I'd been accepted at university. And now I'd thrown it all away for this.

'I guess it's as good a place as any to start.' We bounded forward, towards the lookout tower. Garlands of colourful flowers were laid around the memorial commemorating the fallen of two World Wars. I walked to the edge and gazed across the water. There were acres of bare ground on either side of us; it was worse than looking for a needle in a haystack. Only the aroma of the sea made me happy.

I stared at my doppelgänger. 'This is a waste of time.'

'Over there,' she shouted as she ran, away from the buildings and the water, out into an empty patch of land. I had no idea what she'd seen, but I followed her anyway. What else was there to do?

'Wait,' I whispered.

She stopped running after two minutes. When I caught up with her, I was breathing heavily and my legs ached. Perhaps they'd been aching all day, and I'd been numb to the sensation until now.

'There's smoke coming from the earth.'

I stared at where she pointed, seeing the wisps of air seeping from the ground.

'Maybe there's an underground spa here?'

'I don't see this as a hotbed of beauty treatments.'

We strode towards the spot. The heat from the earth warmed the ankles. Whatever was happening down there, I doubted it was natural. I leant down next to the pockets of air oozing from the mud.

And that's when my foot disappeared into the earth.

Then I followed it.

7 GOING UNDERGROUND

Cassie grabbed my arm before I sank further, pulling me up. Mud covered my leg, joining the stink of dead flesh lingering there. Worms clung to me. I picked them off and laid them on the grass.

'Is this swampland?' Cassie said as she watched me.

'If it is, it's not natural, not for this part of the country. Something has caused the ground to behave like that.'

Cassie dug her foot in the soil.

'There's metal here.'

She knelt and got her hands dirty. When she'd finished, grass and mud covered her skin. Beneath her was a circular iron cover.

'Let's see if we can get this off.' She dug her fingers into the side. I did the same as we pulled upwards. It must have been opened recently as it came away with little effort. Steam drifted out with the unmistakable reek of a sewer.

Cassie pointed at the rungs down the side. 'We should climb down.'

I covered my face with my arm. 'After you.'

Cassie didn't hesitate. I followed her, hauling the cover

over the hole. Tiny feet skittered through the water as I hit the concrete at the bottom. My eyes adjusted to the gloom, but I couldn't get the stink from my nose. I crushed the surge in my throat before I threw up.

She placed her arm on my shoulder. 'Which way should we go, maybe-sister?'

I scowled at the term. She laughed at me. We were at an intersection below the island, with three different directions to choose from. I glanced at each of them, not seeing the flickering light before me, but the terrain above.

'I'm guessing left, which will take us back towards the village.'

Cassie wasn't convinced. 'Wouldn't a clandestine organisation prefer to keep their activities away from the rest of the population?'

'If it were me, I'd want to be close to all the amenities.'

She shrugged and strode ahead. It might have been her natural inclination to lead, but I didn't mind following. I hoped it would reduce the stench assaulting me. The tunnel was damp and narrow, not wide enough for us to walk side-by-side. Rats scampered away as we walked.

'I hope you're not scared of spiders.' She pointed at the large mass of cobwebs covering the walls. Insects never bothered me, even though spiders are arachnids. I'd been to so many schools where people got that wrong, including the teachers, I'd given up trying to correct them.

'Have you thought about what we'll do if we find this group?' I doubted we'd discover anything beyond rat droppings.

Cassie stopped. Her breathing was low, her voice quiet. She turned to me, our faces only inches apart. This close together, it was like staring into a living mirror. The damage to her ear fascinated me. She fascinated me, though I wouldn't admit that to her.

'They'll tell us everything they know about the supernatural. And maybe why the monsters are coming for you.'

It was strange to see such intensity on a face which was and wasn't mine.

'I admire your confidence.'

Then she told me about her plan. A few minutes later, the tunnel opened out into a larger walkway.

Cassie paused. 'Can you hear that?' Her eyes were alert, fingers drifting towards the blade in her jacket. All I heard was the thumping of my heart pounding through my chest and into my skull. 'There are voices up ahead.' She clutched on to the knife.

'Wouldn't it be easier fighting monsters if you had a gun?'

She laughed under her breath. 'I wish, maybe-sister. This isn't America, you know.'

I heard the sounds moving ahead of her as she squinted at me.

'We need to have a serious talk when we leave here.'

'You'll never leave here, girls.'

I twisted to face the owner of that voice, my hand reaching for the knife Cassie had given me a lifetime ago. Before I got it, something sharp bit into my neck. A small needle kissed my skin, and my legs buckled. My shoulder cracked into the wall, and I slipped into the puddles. The last thing I saw as the lights went out was Cassie falling and the spiders skittering towards me.

I FELT like crap when I woke. My mouth was drier than a desert as I reached for the spot where I'd been shot, my fingers finding a small bruise on my skin. I appeared to be collecting injuries at a rapid rate. Lethargy seeped through me, and tiny weights had replaced my bones. Something horrible sneaked up my throat, and I had to stop myself from gagging. Perhaps I'd swallowed some of those spiders.

'You're suffering from the withdrawal effects of the potion we shot you with. I'm sorry about that.' I ignored the pain rushing through me and glared at the woman sitting opposite. I don't know what shook me more: the fact she looked as if she should be in a nursing home or that she was knitting a Christmas jumper. 'It's months before Santa comes, but I always like to start this early. You never know when an emergency will pop up and swallow all your free time.'

'Is Santa real?' I don't know why those words flew from my mouth, but they did.

She laughed and knitted simultaneously. 'Well, he is to my grandchildren.' As she grinned, the light made her shock of grey hair shimmer.

'Where's my...?' I stopped before using the word sister. 'Where's the girl who was with me in the tunnel?'

'Don't worry, she's safe and will join us soon.'

'Who are you?' I flexed my knuckles and scanned the place. It was large, the walls littered with books apart from the spot near the older woman's head, which was decorated with a hefty ornate painting of an ominous-looking man who seemed vaguely familiar.

'I'm Dr Rivers, but you can call me Ellen. That picture behind me is my ancestor Dr Dee. It was he who created the Nexus.'

As I listened to her, I scrutinised every part of the room, trying to locate an exit, but finding nothing.

'What's the Nexus?' Strength returned to my legs and arms. I could take this woman hostage and demand to see Cassie; one of those sharp knitting needles stuck into her cheek should do the trick.

She placed them on her lap as she spoke.

'This is the Nexus around you. It's an accumulation of centuries of knowledge about every non-human thing. I and the others are only the guardians of the information.' She held out her arms and pointed at the mass of books surrounding us.

'It's the twenty-first century, Ellen; you should've digitised all this by now.'

She returned to her knitting. 'Some of my younger colleagues have clamoured for the same thing, but I have to keep warning them about the dangers.'

'What dangers?'

She pursed her lips. 'It's far too easy for electronic files to disappear or be stolen and end up in the wrong hands.' She peered at the books again. 'To get to this treasure, someone would have to break into here.' She returned her attention to me. 'Like you and your sister did.'

'She's not my sister. I hardly know her.' I didn't know why I snapped those words out.

Ellen didn't appear offended. 'Which one of you is the Buffy?'

I arched my eyebrows. 'Buffy?'

'The girl who kills monsters. The rumours of her exploits have gathered over the last six months, but we don't know her name. Some comedian in our weapons department christened her Buffy after the TV show. The description we have of her fits both of you, unless you've been taking turns at it?'

Before I replied, a section of books slid to one side and revealed a doorway. Cassie walked through it, looking unhappy. Behind her came a young bloke with a shock of curly blond hair resembling exploding popcorn, plus a similar-aged stick-thin woman with a morose expression.

'Who do I need to punch for shooting me full of this crappy drug?' Cassie glared at the woman with the knitting needles.

Dr Rivers answered her question.

'It wasn't a drug, but the blood of a sleep kelpie.' Her voice was stern. 'It was justifiable since you're intruders here.' Then she smiled and turned on the charm. 'I'm Dr Ellen Rivers. And what are your names?'

Cassie stared at me for a second. It was time to put our plan into action, so I approached our host.

'We came here to share information with you.'

The popcorn haired man snorted at me. 'What information can kids give us?'

Cassie gave me a nod. It was time to be honest with these people.

'I'm Alice, and that's Cassie. We only met yesterday. Since then, I've been attacked, apparently by werewolves and zombies, but I don't believe in such things. What I defended myself against were infected individuals and others born with an unusual but explainable genetic condition. So I came here hoping someone would provide answers to what's happened.'

Cassie stepped forward. 'And I've been dealing with this craziness for two years.'

Ellen Rivers didn't move, but her chair did; it was electric and glided in silence towards those who'd brought Cassie into this strange library.

'This is Jenny Blaze and her brother, Tom.'

'I'm the brains of the outfit.' Jenny Blaze held her hand out to me, but I ignored it. Her brother grunted.

'The Nexus is a small organisation dedicated to curating all the knowledge gathered about the supernatural since Dr Dee created it at the end of the sixteenth century,' Dr Rivers continued. 'In the early days, the group took more direct action with the supernatural. But over time, as our numbers declined, we've become more about observing, much to the chagrin of some.' The Blaze siblings frowned together. 'What you see here is our accumulated written data, but a few of us, including Jenny, have most of it memorised.'

I glanced at the thousands of documents and books before turning my attention to Jenny Blaze.

'You must have some memory.'

The skinny woman with the dark bob grinned at me.

'My brain is like a computer hardware drive, storing all kinds of useless information.'

'Jenny is too modest.' Rivers glided next to her. 'Her memory is a treasure.'

Tom Blaze approached me. 'How old are you?'

His sister laughed. 'My dear brother, you never ask a lady such a question.'

He sneered in my face. 'I doubt either of these kids is a lady.'

I clenched my fists as Rivers interjected before Cassie thumped him.

'There's an obvious mystery surrounding these two identical ladies, one I guess even they don't have all the answers to, but we can come to that later. First, let's show Alice and Cassie our other treasures.'

Tom Blaze turned to her. 'Are you sure?'

'Yes, Thomas. It should be full disclosure if we're to work together from now on.' She moved towards the gap in the wall where Cassie had entered. 'If you'd follow me.'

Jenny did so without hesitation as Tom lingered back. I went to Cassie and whispered in her ear.

'What do you think?'

She didn't lower her voice. 'These people are no threat to us.'

We followed, my fingers resting on the bruise on my neck, and I wondered how true that was. Tom kept a respectable distance behind us as we entered a long corridor. It appeared to be a hospital ward without the aroma of antiseptic and the smell of impending death. The walls were white and as blank as fresh paper. Cassie was stony-faced as we strode behind the two women in front.

After a minute, Jenny dropped back to speak to us.

'There's a split in the group, in the Nexus, regarding the best way to move forward against supernatural threats.' She projected warmth in everything she did; her body was ungainly when she moved, like a marionette with broken strings, but kindness beamed from her. Her brother appeared to be the complete opposite, skulking a few feet behind.

'What type of split?' Cassie said.

Jenny addressed us both. 'We're having trouble with our funding, and there's conflict about how to deal with the creatures. There's mention of Dr Rivers being forced out.'

I kept my eyes on the doctor as she rolled ahead. 'Has she been here long?'

'Forty years ago, Dr Rivers was on holiday in the Highlands of Scotland when a wendigo attacked her. The creature bit through her leg and, as she lay on the floor, she watched it eat her girlfriend alive.'

Cold ran through me as I stared at the back of the grey-haired woman.

'Why didn't it kill her?' Cassie said.

'What's a wendigo?' I said.

Jenny answered my question first. 'A wendigo is a monster which eats humans, and then takes on their appearance.'

Cassie didn't seem convinced by the story. 'Isn't it native to the Great Lakes region of the US and Canada? What was one doing in the wilds of Scotland?'

'It was never caught, so we don't know why it was there.'

'It didn't kill me because it wanted a mate.'

I had to stop myself from falling on top of Ellen Rivers.

'That sounds horrific and creepy.' Cassie frowned at her.

Tom Blaze's voice made me jump. 'A wendigo legend says if one bites you and leaves you alive, you'll change into one of them.'

'Just like a werewolf.' Cassie's words reminded me of what had happened in the park and the café, sending a shiver down my spine.

'There is a correlation between the wendigo folklore and werewolves,' Jenny said.

'Folklore is based on popular myths. This doesn't sound like that.' I wanted a rational explanation for what I'd heard. 'Are you claiming it left you alive because this thing, whatever attacked you, expected you to change into the same creature, and then it would return to claim you as its wife?'

Cassie laughed. 'Sounds like every boy I've ever met.' She gave Tom Blaze a hard stare.

Dr Rivers looked at me. 'That was the conclusion we came to.'

'So this is all a trick to lure us down here so you can eat Cassie and me?'

Rivers's smile made her look a lot younger than she must have been. 'We could have eaten you when the kelpie blood swam through your veins.' I couldn't tell if she was joking or not.

Cassie got straight to the point. 'So, why aren't you a wendigo?'

Dr Rivers rolled the trouser up on her right leg. The silver prosthetic was shiny in the light.

'This goes to my hip, but the wendigo only bit into my shin.'

'Someone cut off part of your leg to stop the spread of the infection?' My admiration for the woman grew by the second.

'Celestine's brother, Solomon, found us. Luckily for me, he was a surgeon who went nowhere without a scalpel.'

I gasped. 'He removed it with only a scalpel?'

'They say it was a long and difficult process, but I was unconscious for most of it, so I don't know. That was my introduction to the supernatural, and within six months, I was working for the Nexus. And now you can gaze upon our collection.'

She turned the chair around and entered a digital code into a box on the wall. The floor fell away, and we tumbled down.

It wasn't falling, though it seemed like it. In reality, it was an elevator that took us down and into the dark. Lights flickered as my hand found the transparent wall, which appeared from nowhere.

The darkness disappeared after a few minutes, replaced with the sight of a deep, vast space. The wall slid away, and Dr Rivers led us into the room. It was as white as the upstairs, but there were two long rows of small cubicles.

'What's this?' I said.

'Some have advised me to separate our specimens to different sides of the island to lessen the risk if the security fails. However, I believe that would be too dangerous for the rest of the island and beyond. Others think we shouldn't keep any of them alive.' She stared at Tom.

He cleared his throat. 'I don't see what benefit we get by keeping them alive. They'll never tell us what we want.'

Rivers shook her head and moved forward. 'A snake never changes its spots.'

Before I could correct her words, I saw what she meant. In the first cubicle on our right, sitting cross-legged on a weathered wooden stool, was a man dressed as a snake; and spots covered the snakeskin. When the green forked tongue slithered at us, I understood it wasn't a costume.

His appearance mesmerised me, but I tore my gaze away and stared at all the other cubicles. They weren't cubicles, but cells.

This place was a prison: a prison for monsters.

8 THE GIRL WHO FIGHTS MONSTERS

My heart sank as I stared around the room. What had we stumbled into?

'According to our records, this is the last Glycon on the planet. Just think what we could learn from it.'

The Glycon ignored her and peered at me with pale green eyes. Was this a case of another rare genetic condition? It could be an extreme version of ichthyosis. My brain buzzed with the possibilities.

Cassie glanced at the cells. 'How many monsters do you have?'

'Two dozen of the most dangerous are stored here. Let me show you.'

Rivers gave us a guided tour, taking us to the next cell. Leaves covered the floor, and even though there was a clear, hard plastic wall between us and it, the smell of urine and faeces drifted out.

I gazed inside, straining to see anything but a hedge, a large log, and a small tree. A lumpy branch jutted from the top of the tree. Then it moved. A monkey uncurled itself from the tree, its shrivelled yellow eyes cutting into me.

When it dropped to the ground, I realised it was no monkey; it had the body of a jet-black shaggy sheepdog.

'This is a Shug Monkey,' Rivers said with pride. 'It was caught terrorising the village of West Wratting in Cambridgeshire before the start of the Second World War. Some of our scholars think a spectre possessed a normal monkey and a hound and created this hybrid.'

The animal listened to her intently, then pushed its arms into the ground and stood on those dog-like legs. It had a huge neck and peered at us through intelligent human-looking eyes. It flared its nostrils and exhibited powerful jaws of a bone-crushing nature. It appeared fierce, but was no monster.

'This is some animal experiment gone wrong, that's all.' My hand was on the cage. 'I'm surprised at you, Dr Rivers; a woman of science should know better than this. Perhaps you're still suffering from the trauma of the attack forty years ago.'

'You'll never convince her,' Cassie said to Rivers.

I wondered if this wasn't all some practical joke on me.

'We'll see,' Rivers said as she moved to the next cell. I couldn't do anything but play along and see what other fakes they had to show me. I stared through the glass, my heart sinking at the sight: a woman looking older than time sat at a table, a broom laid at her feet. She turned towards us, elongated pencil-thin arms outstretched in supplication. Her nose was as long as her arms, resembling the withered branch of an ancient tree. She was clothed in a lengthy blue dress covered in grass stains. When her mouth opened, tiny flies sputtered out, and she spoke in a language I didn't recognise.

I turned to Rivers, fire burning inside my eyes and my cheeks.

'Why have you imprisoned this sickly old woman?'

Rivers shook her head at me. 'It's not human. That's a Baba Yaga, a forest-dwelling creature that eats children. We think it came over here on a Russian ship in the early 1840s. When kids went missing in Kielder Forest in the late 1880s, one of our explorer teams tracked it down and caught it.'

My fingers shook, eyebrows twitching beyond my control. These people were crazed, possibly a cult. I glanced at Cassie, expecting her to feel the way I did, but she seemed happy with what surrounded us.

I staggered up to the next cell, pulling at the top of my shirt and trying to breathe. I didn't want to look inside, turning my head to frown at Cassie.

She looked puzzled. 'This is empty.'

Cassie was right. There was nothing but a vacant bed covered in a black and white sheet. My heart slowed as fingers gripped my palm. And then my eyes played tricks on me as the dark part of the cover shimmered like water and slipped on to the floor.

'Damn,' Cassie said as the darkness took shape, forming arms, a head and body, plus legs. Its face was blank, devoid of form or light.

Rivers glided next to us. 'I'm guessing you girls have never seen a Shadow Person. Or perhaps you have, and you didn't realise it.'

The dark entity stood a few feet away behind the clear wall, and I was glad the barrier was there. Its fingers trembled like liquid, and a shiver trickled down my spine. I fought my fear and moved closer, my face pressing up to the plastic, its coldness adding to the chill swarming over me. What was this thing? Had someone dressed all in black in an effects suit?

Then, without warning, it sprang at me, hitting the

obstacle separating us. I stumbled, falling into Jenny Blaze; her brother screwed up his eyes and laughed at me.

I clung to his sister. 'What... what is it?'

Jenny held my hand and steadied my racing nerves.

'We don't know where the Shadow People come from. Some say they're negative aspects of us released into the world after we die, or possibly a soul split asunder from the body using dark magic. All we know is how dangerous they are. This one killed four people before we contained it.'

The shadow shape slid down the barrier and into a puddle on the floor. Then it reformed into a human silhouette, but this time it had a face, with large white eyes scrutinising me. It was the only other shade on its body; until light shapes like tears ran down its cheeks.

I'd had enough of this sideshow, desperate to get away and above ground. It had been a mistake to listen to Cassie and go there. I needed to go back and face the consequences from the police and Artemis. My studies were all that mattered.

Cassie moved to the next cell. 'Unbelievable.'

Rivers and her helpers went past me. 'We have some extraordinary creatures in our vaults, but the cyclops is one of the most impressive,' she said.

Against my better judgement, I joined them. A giant of a man, maybe eight feet tall, was chained against the wall, clothed in tattered rags, but his face was his most distracting feature, a single eye staring from above his forehead. There were cuts across his cheeks and over his hands.

I smacked my hand against the cage. 'This man should be in a hospital, not shackled like a beast.'

I turned away from them, volcanic lava flowing through my veins and making my head throb. There were at least another twelve cells, and it sickened me to consider what was inside them. We only had this woman's word that these prisoners were dangerous.

She faced me. 'I get the impression you disapprove of this, Alice. I believe your sister might disagree.'

I pulled Cassie to one side, ignoring the sister comment. 'This isn't right, Cassie. They've created a freak show full of captives with unusual medical conditions. It's like a Victorian sideshow.'

Cassie twisted her face. 'Don't be naïve, Alice. These things will kill people without hesitation.' She turned to Rivers. 'You have more dangerous ones somewhere else?'

Rivers grinned from ear to ear. 'We do, but can you tell me what you've encountered on your travels?'

Cassie never hesitated. 'Werewolves, zombies, trolls, gremlins, a golem, a ghoul, a banshee, a boggart. Recently there's been a bunch of demons.'

'Demons?' Rivers appeared confused. She glanced at the Blaze siblings. 'We didn't know such things existed. The Nexus always believed they, like heavenly creatures, were only myths.'

Cassie leant into the glass separating her from the cyclops. 'In the last six months, I've had to deal with four of them. It's as if something has agitated the supernatural world and loosened them from the Hell they were hiding in.'

'How do you know they were demons?' I said.

'They were keen to tell me when they thought they had the upper hand. They're much stronger than humans, but I was cleverer.'

'What do they look like?' Rivers's voice trembled as she spoke.

'They hide inside people, but the ones I killed, when

they revealed their true selves, were the ruby-skinned horned beasts of legend.'

Dr Rivers moved to the Blaze siblings. They knelt to her level, and the three of them whispered furiously.

Cassie's eyes flared red. 'They know less than I do.'

Jenny broke away from the others and came to us. 'We need to take you upstairs.'

'Why?' Cassie appeared to be in no mood to follow anymore.

'We have to speak to the Oracle.' Dr Rivers appeared shaken, her eyes wide and nervous. 'She might help with this demon thing, and might know something about the mystery of you two.'

'No.' Cassie's voice was calm. 'We'll get our answers somewhere else.'

She strode towards the lift. I wanted to leave, but also had to free the unfortunate people imprisoned there.

'I told you they were useless to us.' Tom Blaze spat out the words as he removed a mobile device from his pocket. 'And they can't be allowed to go.' He pressed into the digital screen.

'No!' Rivers and Jenny Blaze shouted together. The cell door closest to the exit slid open. I was frozen to the spot as a reptilian fist slammed into Cassie's face.

I leapt forward as the Glycon stepped from his cage.

'I'll slllaughttter thesssse chillldrennn, annddd theeenn feasssst onnn yourrrr bonesss, Riverrrsss.'

Long claws reached for Cassie's throat as I crashed into his legs. The force took both of us tumbling back into the cell.

'Close the door!' I screamed.

It banged shut as scaly fingers grabbed my neck.

'Youlll dooo forrr nowww.'

The stink of sulphur dripped from the Glycon's lips as cold scales clutched at my flesh. I kicked out and pushed him away.

I needed a weapon, scanning the cell for something, but finding nothing. I backed up against the barrier. There was a large block of wood between us. From the corner of my eye, I saw Cassie and Tom Blaze struggling on the floor. Where was the security?

The Glycon's eyes were fixed on me, frozen inside the green flesh. I couldn't win a physical fight with him. Artemis had sent me to a conflict management course last year, and it was time to put the theory into practice.

'My name is Alice; what's yours?' There was nothing but silence and a deathly stare. 'How long have they kept you a prisoner here?' Defensive measures raced through my head. The Glycon wasn't bulky or much taller than me, but his arms were sinewy, and his muscles quivered as he flexed them. His nails were more like talons, sharpened and ready to tear out my flesh.

I slid down the wall and sat cross-legged opposite him to make myself as non-threatening as possible. Water filled his eyes, which blinked in confusion. Behind me were the sounds of fighting.

'Is it true what Dr Rivers said: are you the last of your kind?' I relaxed my body as much as possible, placing my hands flat and up to expose my palms.

Time appeared to move in slow motion; it couldn't have been more than two minutes since I'd been locked in the cage, but it seemed like an eternity. My heart thumped in my ears, so loud I thought it had crawled from my chest to get there.

Was this Glycon playing with me, tormenting his food before feasting?

'Myyy nameee isss Sssarrdaa.' Saliva dripped from his mouth. 'I havvve beeen lockeeed awwwayy for sssooo lonnng, I cannnt reeemmeemmbeer whheeenn ittt wassss.'

Sadness gripped my heart. This was no monster, and I wasn't the one trapped here. I had to get both of us out of there. As I considered how to do that, something barged into the cage at my back.

'I promise I'll help you, Sarda.' I stood and turned to see the confusion outside. Tom Blaze had Cassie pinned to the ground, his eyes consumed by mania and anger, his knee thrust into her gut. I had to get out.

Behind me came the sound of scaled feet moving across the floor. Sarda's breath was hot and sticky on my neck, his hand cold and wet on my shoulder. I was an inch away from having my throat ripped out.

'Thhhe worrssst monsssteerr innn heeeree isss thhhat boy.'

Blaze's hands were around Cassie's neck; his sister and Rivers were nowhere. I bashed my fists on to the plastic and howled. Blaze turned to me and winked. It was the distraction Cassie needed. She brought her fingers up and into his Adam's apple, following with her palm into his jaw. He collapsed in a heap, and the electronic lock to the cell tumbled from his pocket. Cassie picked it up and let me out.

'Are you okay?' I jumped forward and lifted her.

'I've had worse.' Cassie spat out a huge cough before peering into space behind me. I turned to stare at Sarda, who had retreated to the back of the cell. Cassie used the electronic device to lock it again. As soon as she did, Rivers and the Blaze girl returned. Jenny rushed to her brother, who was unconscious on the floor.

'What happened to you two?' I didn't hide my anger, but Rivers was indifferent to it.

'If a holding room is opened without authorisation, the protocol is to leave immediately.'

Jenny Blaze tried to revive her brother. I wanted to punch him in the face.

'This is some operation you have,' Cassie said sarcastically.

'Don't you have security for this?' I wondered what type of two-bit joint we'd stumbled into.

Rivers moved towards the lift with no second glance at the Blaze siblings.

'If you girls would follow me, I'll take you to someone who might answer your questions.'

Jenny stopped cajoling her brother and peered at the back of the Doctor's head. Cassie and I glanced at each other.

'You can't take them to see Bella.' All concern for her brother had vanished.

Rivers paused outside the lift, facing the three of us.

'I'm in charge of this facility. You deal with him, and I'll speak to you later.'

The girl grunted as the door opened. Cassie strode ahead as I looked at Sarda. The last surviving Glycon peered into my eyes, and I wondered how I'd keep my promise to him.

Cassie was as cold as ice. 'You'd have let Alice die and left me with that thug of yours?'

'We observed everything on the monitors, how you dealt with Thomas, and how your sister handled the Glycon. We never knew its name until now, so it was all beneficial.'

'We're not sisters,' Cassie said.

'Whatever you are, you're naturals at this.' Rivers looked at me. 'It was remarkable what you did, Alice, to gain control over the monster.'

'Why do you have Sarda imprisoned here?'

Cassie frowned, but Rivers smiled.

'The creature has been here longer than me. Our records show it murdered a family on the shore of Loch Ness in 1932. I understand the consensus at the time was to destroy it as we'd done with all the other monsters captured over the centuries. Still, my predecessor implemented a policy of containment and study.'

'Which is why you have this collection?' I hated using that word.

'You should kill them all.' Cassie ground her teeth as she spoke.

Rivers looked horrified. 'Oh no, we can't do that. We've learnt so much from our menagerie over the years, none more so than the one we'll see now.'

'This Bella is a prisoner?' I struggled to control my annoyance as we descended. 'Why haven't you kept her with the others?'

'You'll see when we meet her.' Rivers stared at Cassie. 'I hope she can give us some information about these demons you've encountered.'

'Why does the idea of demons bother you?' It seemed a silly thing to ask, but I did anyway.

'As I mentioned, we have records on supernatural creatures and incidents going back five hundred years, and there is no mention of any encounters with demons. All we have are myths and legends of folklore and superstition.'

We came to a halt with a bump. The door slid open, and we followed Rivers out. The place reminded me of a drawing room or a library from an Agatha Christie novel, full of dusty books, antique furniture and a piano sitting in the corner. Portrait paintings of distinguished-looking gentlemen and women covered the walls, apart from the far one, which had a coffin nailed into it a few feet above the carpet.

Rivers pointed at the canvases. 'These are my predecessors. Once I'm gone, my likeness will join them.' I imagined the sorrow in her voice was not due to the thought of her death, but the fear this organisation would have to survive without her. 'But I haven't brought you here to peer at dusty pictures of people long dead; we need to talk to Bella.' She wheeled her way to the end of the room and the coffin pinned to the wall.

Cassie pulled me close.

'I don't trust any of these lunatics.' Her eyes scanned the place. 'I haven't seen a way out apart from where we came in, so be on your guard.'

'Yes, maybe-sister,' I whispered to her, amused by her furrowed reaction. It was hard to tell if she wanted us to be related or not.

We moved to stand on either side of Dr Rivers. She pressed something concealed in her wheelchair, and the front of the hanging coffin slid open.

It was a peculiar sight: skull and bony hands were what I noticed first, the rest of the body hidden by an impressive blue pinstriped suit. Thick metal chains pinned the bones to the wall over the arms, wrists, ankles and thighs.

'I'm told Bella's clothes would fetch a small fortune on the antique apparel market. Well, they would, apart from one minor problem.'

What she meant by a minor problem was the large piece of wood sticking out of Bella's heart.

9 BELLA

'You staked a vamp?' Cassie sounded impressed.

Rivers shook her head. 'It was pure luck on our part. It was during the Blitz in London in 1940. Have either of you heard of the tragedy at Balham Underground station?'

Cassie said no, but I had. History was another one of my favourite hobbies.

'On the 14th of October 1940, a bomb hit the station and exploded above the cross passage between the two platforms. The water and gas mains and the sewage pipes broke: water flooded the tunnels below, and gas hampered rescue efforts. Over sixty people died, another seventy injured. Most of the casualties resulted from the blast and debris.' Black and white images of the devastation flashed through my mind.

Rivers was unmoved. 'Well, when the authorities began recovering the bodies, they discovered Bella. They summarised that the explosion sent this piece of wood through her heart. They were confused regarding the speed of decomposition of the body, but some bright spark put it down to a secret Nazi weapon. Somebody was ready to remove the stake when a rescuer commented on her clothes.'

'What about her clothes?' They appeared normal to me.

'Well, unless you were Marlene Dietrich, a woman wearing a suit was unusual in those days. I guess it was more unfamiliar than the impossibility of a body turning to the bone so quickly. One of them even mentioned Dietrich's name - I've listened to the taped interviews hundreds of times - which got people talking about German spies, and they all panicked. It was up to the local copper to restore some calm to the situation.'

'What did he do?'

'He checked her pockets.' Rivers moved from the hanging coffin towards the desk at her side. She entered a four-digit number at the front of one drawer and opened it. She took an envelope and handed it to me. 'This is what he found.'

I removed the paper from inside and stared at the unknown symbols. Then, I showed it to Cassie.

She frowned. 'What is this?'

'It's a code. The rescuers panicked as they assumed it was the plans of a Nazi spy cell, preparing for an invasion. Luckily, the beat copper had his head screwed on. He made sure the body was not disturbed and told his superiors. They informed the Government, who passed it on to the SOE, and the details found their way to us. It was all rather fortuitous.'

Cassie scratched her chin. 'Who are the SOE?'

More history facts returned to me. 'The Special Operations Executive was a British World War II organisation. Its purpose was to conduct espionage, sabotage, reconnaissance against the Axis powers, and aid local resistance movements.'

'Like James Bond.' Cassie licked her lips.

I stared at the paper, concentrating on the first lines of the text.

'Do you know what it says?'

The Doctor shook her head. 'No. Hundreds of people have looked at it over the years. The code breakers at Bletchley Park even studied it, but we still don't understand what any of it means.'

'Meet at the Thames. Prepare for the Forthcoming. Something like that.'

Rivers's eyes nearly popped from her head. 'You can read it?'

'Only a few words: Prepare, Thames and Forthcoming stand out. I added the rest to make sense.'

'How can you do that, Alice?' Cassie brimmed with admiration.

'I've always been good at puzzles and creating codes. I created my own languages when I was younger to stop people from reading my diaries.'

'Do you think you could decipher the whole thing?' Rivers practicality begged me to help her. But after what had happened upstairs, I was in no mood to assist her, or anyone else in this organisation.

'Maybe,' I said without committing myself.

'Bella has never explained what it is, what it means. She's said many things, but nothing about that, and very little about her history.'

'What has she told you?' I wondered what trick they'd pull with this coffin and its skeleton. I didn't believe a word about rescuers finding this at Balham Station during the Blitz. This operation was one big sham, but I couldn't understand what they were getting out of it; government funding, maybe. Plenty of unethical scientists had done the same thing over the years. If the finances were running out, then perhaps they were desperate for money.

'Bella has given us many secrets of the supernatural,' Rivers said. 'And that's why I'm hoping she can tell us something about these demons. She claims to be hundreds of years old. So which one of you would like to do the honours?'

I stared at her in confusion, unsure of what she meant. Cassie shrugged.

'I'll do it.'

'Don't respond to what she says unless I tell you to, and under no circumstances reveal anything personal about yourselves, this place, or what year this is.'

'Are you that scared of a woman chained inside a coffin?' Cassie said.

'Don't think of her as human. Remove the stake, and she'll live again.'

'I've always decapitated vampires, so I don't know about this.' Cassie's hand was on the wood. I expected her to remove it slowly and then edge back towards me, but she yanked it out in one go and didn't move from the spot.

The air was sucked from the room as static electricity swirled around. My fingers touched Cassie's, tiny sparks flying between us, and the hairs along my arms bounced to attention. It was the skeleton's hand that changed first, atrophy in reverse as blood and muscle and skin appeared from nothing, glued in layers to the corpse shackled to the wall. It was an impressive effect. When the hands were fully formed, my focus turned to the head. The smell of fried bananas invaded the room as flesh sprang from the skull like an animation going backwards.

I had a sudden flash of memory from my childhood of watching an old Hammer horror movie where the hero staked the vampire, and his skin melted away; this was the exact opposite. I dragged Cassie back as volume pushed its way into the pinstriped suit. A powerful popping sound burst into the room as two fully formed eyeballs appeared from nothing and gazed straight at me.

'Oh my God!' Cassie and I spoke as one.

Ruby hued veins grew around the eyes before sinking into the cheekbones. Eyelids sprang like flowering shrubs and blinked at me. Wide-open lips and immaculate teeth grinned outwards. The whole thing was over in fewer than two minutes. The woman who had been a suit of bones had straight blonde hair down to her shoulders and sparkling opals for eyes. I was falling beneath that sapphire gaze when her voice snapped me from my reverie.

'How nice it is to see you again, Ellen. You look tired and old, my dear.' Her words were like a gossamer thread floating on velvet wings. 'And you've brought new people for me to chat with; how wonderful.' Her eyes dug into Cassie and me. She reached her hand out, but the chains restricted her. 'I'm Bella, and you two are?'

'Bella isn't your real name,' Dr Rivers said. 'You've refused to say who you are.'

Bella pulled her hand back. 'That's why one of your witty crew named me after Mr Lugosi. How charming of them. I met him once, Lugosi, to tell him how disappointed I was with his portrayal. He was so drunk, he didn't believe I was real.' Her laugh rattled my bones. She twisted her head towards Rivers. 'What a shame you didn't bring that strange boy, Thomas, with you.'

Rivers's face crumpled in surprise. 'How do you know of him?'

Bella stared at the ceiling as if she was preparing for a night on the town.

'Didn't Thomas mention our regular get-togethers? That must be why he turns off all the recording equipment you have in here.'

'You're lying,' Rivers said.

'I think the poor boy has a crush on me, the way he's always picking dust from my trousers and letting his fingers linger on my legs.'

Dr Rivers moved across the room, away from Bella to the desk from which she'd removed the envelope earlier. Bella returned her attention to us.

'None of them, even troubled Thomas, will tell me what year it is. I don't know what they're so fearful of, but to witness young women wearing trousers of the most unusual material gives me great hope of the progress made since that pesky piece of wood flew across the station and into my heart. I'm guessing you two are identical twins.' She leant forward and sniffed the air. 'Though there is something different about both of you. I can't quite put my finger on what it is. Still, I can't put my fingers on most things in this position.' Her laugh was lilting and addictive.

Dr Rivers finished what she was doing and re-joined us in front of Bella.

'There are no records from the last five years of anyone speaking to you apart from me.' There was control in her voice, but she couldn't hide the annoyance in her face. 'I'm wise to your games, Bella. You can cooperate, or the stake will return you to bones.'

'Quid pro quo, Ellen; you know how this works. You give me what I need, and I'll consider answering your questions.'

'You'll get it after you do as we ask.'

It appeared to be a standoff until Bella agreed. 'You always drive a hard bargain, Ellen. The least you can do is introduce me to your unusual friends.' She had a smile to illuminate the night.

Rivers ignored her demand. 'What do you know about demons?'

Bella lifted her hand as if she wanted to touch her cheek before remembering she couldn't reach it.

'I haven't encountered a demon since Henry VIII's wedding party for Anne Boleyn.'

'You're that old?' I wondered how far they'd take this charade.

'I'm even older, kid.' She winked at me.

'So, they are real?' Rivers said. Cassie scowled at her, a look which said why believe this creature and not me?

'They are very much real, Ellen, but they retreated from the human world at the end of the sixteenth century.'

'Do you know why?' I said.

Bella wiggled her nose. 'The rumour was they were preparing for something, strengthening their forces for the return of an old enemy.'

Silence engulfed the room.

'Do you mean the Forthcoming?' I said.

The so-called vampire's eyes narrowed and her lips trembled.

'What do you know about that, child?'

'She unlocked your code, Bella.' Rivers held the paper with the secret symbols in her hand, pointing it at the woman in chains.

Bella regained her composure and peered at me. 'I wonder if you can unlock the secrets of your life.' She looked at Rivers. 'It's your turn.'

Rivers hesitated for a second before turning her chair

and heading towards the stack of books in the far corner. As she did so, Bella spoke to us.

'She'll read me a bedtime story.' She ran her tongue over her top lip. 'If you kids let me go, I'll tell you a secret about the two of you.'

'Vampires don't exist,' I said.

Cassie frowned at me, and then pushed her face so close to Bella, I thought they might kiss.

'You're lying again as you did earlier about the Blaze kid.'

I wanted to pull her back, suddenly bereft of scientific certainty, afraid if Bella were a real vampire, even in chains, she'd lean forward and thrust her teeth into Cassie's neck.

'I'm many things, but a liar isn't one of them. The troublesome boy visits me regularly. I could have kept quiet about it, could have bided my time and charmed him into setting me free, but I sense that time is running out for all of us.'

Cassie stepped to my side. Before we could reply, Dr Rivers returned. She had a glass of dark liquid in her hand. She held it up for Bella to drink. Even before she devoured it, I knew what it was from the aroma: fresh blood.

'Ah,' Bella said as she finished it. 'That's nearly an arm full.'

I glared at Rivers.

'It's lamb's blood,' she said as she grabbed the empty glass.

Bella used her tongue to wipe the red stain from her mouth. 'Who's lying now?'

'Come,' Rivers said, 'we got what we needed. You can put the stake back.'

Cassie lifted the wood towards the strange woman in the coffin.

'You two are an experiment,' Bella said.

Cassie froze.

'What do you mean?' I said.

Bella curled her lips, the blood lingering there. 'All life on this planet began with twos, and you girls are the apotheosis of an eternity of experiments.'

'Is this another lie?' Dr Rivers said.

Bella puffed out her cheeks. 'In the beginning, there was the union of one plus one: two humans, two vampires, two dogs, two cats, two mermaids, two dragons, and so on. A multitude of creatures sent out into the world to either flourish or suffer.'

'That sounds like a science experiment focused on reproduction,' I said.

'Indeed, but its long-term aim was to produce siblings of great influence.' Bella spoke to us all, but stared at me.

Her gaze worried me. 'What does that mean?'

'You'll never know if you stick that piece of wood in me.'

Cassie pressed the stake into the suit, close to Bella's chest, but not quite in. She pushed her ear to Bella's face, and the chained woman's lips moved. Bella spoke, but I didn't hear her words. Then Cassie plunged the stake through the clothes and into Bella's heart. A small gasp drifted from her mouth as the flesh shrivelled from her. Cassie and I stepped back as Bella returned to a suit of bones. Was it all an effect? It had to be, didn't it, just like everything else in here? But Sarda was real. I'd recognised the pain in his eyes, understood the loneliness.

'What did she say to you?' Rivers said to Cassie.

'She said I was the best looking one in the room.'

Dr Rivers moved to the desk. 'We need to find out what she meant about you two.' She took a phone from her jacket and sent a text.

Cassie's hand was on the wood sticking out of Bella's ribs.

'You mean all that nonsense about being separated at birth as part of a secret experiment, to study us as if someone or some group has recorded everything we've done since?'

Rivers put her phone on the desk. 'The one thing I've learnt in this life is that nothing is impossible.'

A sudden terrible thought slammed against the inside of my skull and gave me a headache.

What if it was true? What if Artemis had used me as a guinea pig all this time?

10 DREAMCATCHER

Every muscle in my body screamed. I touched the cut on my forehead, wondered if the bruise around my eye was still there, questioned if my place in the world was as it should be. Cassie placed her hand on my arm.

'You're worried about Artemis?' It was as if she'd read my mind.

Rivers perched her chair in front of us. 'Who is Artemis?'

I started to explain it to her, but Cassie stopped me. 'That's not important. All that matters is removing this stake again and getting her to tell us what she meant.'

'She won't help you. What happened to the two of you when you were born is hidden in your memories. Both of you need to access what you've suppressed.'

As Rivers finished speaking, the door to the lift opened, and Jenny Blaze walked out. She carried a small box in her hand.

'My earliest memory is from when I was five or six,' I said, 'and I don't see how cutting my knee on a piece of glass would help anyone.'

I still remembered how the broken bottle cut through my flesh and how the blood felt as it trickled down my skin. I recalled how the woman in charge of the foster home threw a plaster at me and told me to fix myself.

Blaze placed the box in front of Rivers. There was no acknowledgement from her about what had happened upstairs as the Doctor put her hand on the container.

'We have to access your dreams, and we need to start with Cassie.'

Cassie snorted laughter. 'Good luck with that, Doc. I haven't had a dream in a long time, so if you're going to hypnotise me, you won't get anything.'

'Everybody dreams. It's the only way the brain can make sense of things. Hypnotism is very limited at separating the truth of memory from the dream it hides inside, which is why we use a Dreamcatcher.'

She unlocked the box and removed its contents. In her palm was a tiny human figure, no bigger than her little finger, which peered at me through watery eyes. I stared at it, transfixed. Was it mechanical?

Cassie pointed at the thing. 'What are you going to do with that?'

Blaze replied, 'The Dreamcatcher works in symbiosis with its host to release the locked memories to experience them all over again. Cassie will then describe them to us as they happen to her.'

'How is this symbiosis achieved?' I didn't like the sound of it, searching for a scientific explanation for what she'd said and the thing in her hand.

Rivers passed the creature to Blaze. 'The Dreamcatcher forms a physical link with Cassie's brain.'

Blaze strode towards Cassie.

'This sounds dangerous.' Adrenaline flooded my

system, saliva thickened in my throat, and sweat trickled over the cut on my head, stinging me like vinegar.

'Do you want the truth or not?' An ugly snarl crept across the Blaze girl's face. The warmth I'd seen in her earlier had vanished.

'Do what you have to,' Cassie said.

Jenny Blaze moved towards her. 'Hold out your hand.'

Cassie did, and Blaze placed the Dreamcatcher in my doppelgänger's palm. I didn't know what to do, fearful, but also fascinated by what was about to happen.

The creature stretched out its arms as one more impossible thing made my head hurt. Its tiny fingers grew longer, like branches on a tree, snaking up towards Cassie's face. I flinched backwards as they slithered into her nose, but Cassie didn't move or utter a sound, until she spoke.

'The Dreamcatcher is with me.'

That name is inappropriate. I deal with memories, not dreams, and I don't catch them but seek them out behind barriers and walls, reveal where they hide deep within the dark and the brightest illuminations. Can you feel my tendrils inside your brain?

It was Cassie's voice, but not her voice; that thing was speaking through her.

'Is that what the wriggling is? It's uncomfortable.' That was Cassie's voice.

You'll get used to it soon.

'How does this work?'

The ends of my fingers contain millions of micro sensors attuned to the parts of the brain which store your memories. It's a case of loosening the more difficult ones in the correct order and without the wrong consequences.

'Is this dangerous, like Alice said?'

Didn't they warn you about losing the tether?

'I've found these Nexus people to be less forthcoming than I expected.'

We'll work together, moving back through your mind, starting with something recent to tether you to this point, until we reach the moment of your birth. But those moments are hidden far in the earliest parts of your life. There's a danger you might get stranded there.

'And that means what, exactly?'

Your consciousness will regress to that point, trapped behind a brain incapable of anything but gurgling. Shall we start?

'Of course.'

Pick a recent event as the tether.

'The image is already there. Only it isn't an image because I'm inside the event once more, observing from the sides. The girl climbs from the lake as the werewolf slips under the water. I gaze at Alice, and she peers at me: the shock surges through me again.'

Good, Cassie. This is perfect as a point to return to. Now let's move further back together.

'I feel you pressing through my synapses, bringing forward flashes of flickering lights and the sweet aroma of oranges and strawberries. I see shelves and rows of fruit and vegetables. This is from two years ago and my first planned mission against the supernatural.'

I feel the coldness in your bones. This isn't fear, but calculated confidence.

'My last foster family lived around the corner. I spent six months with them. He was a secret drug addict, and she was a control freak. But that wasn't why I was in his shop. Three kids had disappeared in the time I was there, and the authorities were clueless why. They were lumped together as troubled teens who turned into runaways, but I knew better.'

And how did you know that?

'The man who owned the shop was a devourer of children.'

A human killer?

'No, he was a supernatural monster. I knew it the first time I saw him when I went to buy some apples.'

How did you know?

'Watch it through my eyes as the shopkeeper steps from behind the counter. On first appearance, he is a small, balding man with beady eyes. His body is thin, malnourished and lacking in strength. But I see the abyss inside him, hear the inhuman beat of his heart, and smell the decay of his flesh. Nobody else witnessed these things, but I did.'

He was a child eater. How were your senses able to determine this?

'I don't know. It had been happening for years, but I hadn't realised what it was. I still don't know why it happens.'

Show me what you did.

'He grinned at me and said he had an iPhone in the back he didn't want. So I followed him inside and down the stairs.'

My heartbeat is matching yours. You are apprehensive, but confident; impressive for one so young.

'The shopkeeper locks the door behind me. His breathing is heavy, and I hear him laughing. I ask what he did with the other kids.

'He rubs his stomach and slavers at me. You'll see them soon, girl, he says. His fingernails extend by six inches, the top row of his teeth growing over his lips like a sabre-tooth tiger. He stinks of rotten fish. He lunges at me in manic glee. I bring my arm up, twisting away from his grasp, and sweep my hand across his face. The blade slices through his throat with ease.'

How were you so skilled at this age?

'It took years of practice.'

Show me. I'll push my fingers deeper into your brain.

'At ten, I suffocate a ghoul masquerading as my social worker. The police recorded it as a heart attack, unable to believe a child slight of frame could harm a grown man in such a way.

'Eight years old, I've run away from another foster home. I stride into the river, intent on getting to the other side and out of town. My feet are cold and wet. There's a stone in my guts.

'A hand below the water grabs at my ankle. I snap away from it, turning to see burning red eyes glaring up. I stamp at it and run through the ripples, my legs struggling against the heavy wetness. Claws scratch my skin.'

That hurts.

'I stamp again, harder this time, hitting flesh and bone where the redness was. The scream erupts from the river as I reach the other side. I scramble through the grass and the mud, running forward and never looking back. But back I go, further and further. The light recedes into nothing. Darkness is all there is. Fear grips the whole of my being.

'Isolation, loneliness, the wrench of separation. A yearning, an inescapable hollowness engulfs me. There is an eternity of tumbling into the abyss.'

You need to pull yourself out of this, Cassie. I'm reaching further back, but if you fall too far, you'll never return.

'I feel you sinking deeper into my brain, sifting through my unconscious and conscious mind. Sharp pain is in my frontal lobe. A voice, somewhere far off, is calling to me. I'm falling, grasping for safety. A blast of electric agony shoots through my leg, my vision returning as I stare at the grass below me. My body trembles as I lift, light reflecting off the shard of glass sticking from my knee. The air smells of burning copper and the fresh blood stuck to the bottom of my skirt.

'I never wear skirts.'

Further back, Cassie.

'I try to pull the glass out, and the scene changes again to brilliant white walls and an aroma of antiseptic. Then a voice I don't recognise. The babies haven't cried once, she says. I can't see the woman speaking. There's a sign on the wall saying St Claire's Hospital.

'It's remarkable the way they look so alike. Do you want to know where they'll go? she says.

'Yes, I say.

'No, of course not. I understand. This is the only way to keep them safe, but what about you? Her voice trembles with fear.

'I wait for the answer, but there is only silence, an absence of sound which drags me further into a vacuum.

'Then there's only a void.'

Cassie stopped speaking as the Dreamcatcher's fingers shrivelled from her face and returned to their normal size. The creature jumped from her hand on to the ground and stamped towards the corner of the room. Jenny Blaze scooped it up in her palm. As she did, Cassie tumbled to the floor. I dropped to my knees and cradled her in my arms. Her eyes were glazed, her lips trembling.

'What's wrong with her?' My emotions were exhausted by what I'd witnessed and heard.

'There's no help for her now.' Tom Blaze pointed a gun at me.

'I thought she would be the stronger of them,' Rivers said. 'Get the Dreamcatcher ready for the other one, Jenny.'

I held on to Cassie as she convulsed and shook in my arms. I glared at Rivers.

'You planned this from the start.'

'You should never have broken into here, Alice. Once I found out how unusual you two are, there was no other outcome but this one. You girls are the most fascinating specimens we've ever acquired.' Rivers held her hand up, stopping Jenny Blaze as she approached me with the Dreamcatcher. 'It might be prudent to wait with that.'

I resisted the urge to remove the smug smile from Rivers's face, and it was nothing to do with Tom Blaze waving the gun at me. I lowered my head into Cassie's, pushing my lips into her ear.

'Listen to me, maybe-sister, find your way back now. Wherever you are, I need you with me.' Her breathing was laboured, her chest rising slowly against my hand.

Jenny returned the Dreamcatcher to its box, whispering something to Rivers as the boy dragged me up. Cold metal pressed against my cheek.

'You can leave her. You'll both be joining your little snake friend soon enough.'

I stared at him. 'What do you mean?'

'I enjoyed killing that green freak, but it will be more fun dealing with you and the lookalike.'

His overconfidence was his downfall. The second he dropped the weapon an inch was the exact moment Cassie came out of her condition. She leapt forward like a spring, grabbed his wrist and pushed him behind me. She grappled with him on the ground as his sister threw the Dream-catcher box at my head. It took me by surprise, catching me on the jaw even though I twisted to the side to avoid it.

Before I could react, Jenny Blaze was on top of me, and we hit the floor next to Cassie and the horrible boy.

'Don't kill them,' Rivers shouted.

The Blaze girl's arm was pushed up against my throat, pressing the life from my lungs. She paid no attention to her leader's demands. Jenny shifted her body, her knee pushing into my gut. Pain erupted inside me as if I'd been plugged into an electricity socket.

Jenny lowered her head to mine, her face consumed by mania. Whatever the psychosis was, it ran in the family.

'Everybody thinks Tom is the crazy one, but they don't realise I hide it better.'

I couldn't breathe, my lungs shrinking as my ribs throbbed against my chest. It was difficult to appreciate the irony of spending the last day fighting off so-called supernatural beasts, only to have my life snuffed out by the most human of monsters.

The pain was so much, I turned numb, but I still felt the tiny feet running up my legs and across my stomach. The light faded from my eyes as the Dreamcatcher launched itself at Jenny's face. Its nails dug into her cheek, and she screamed. The survival instinct should have forced her to let go of me to swat her attacker away, but she didn't. It was all the Dreamcatcher needed, releasing one of its hands, its fingers growing with great speed and penetrating her nostrils.

'I'll distract her,' the Dreamcatcher said to me. 'You save your twin.'

I didn't need telling twice. I leapt from the floor and jumped on the boy, wrenching him from where he was strangling Cassie. We rolled over the ground like tumbleweeds joined at the hip, coming to a stop only a few feet from Rivers. Tom's gun was next to the wheel of her electronic chair. The murderous boy let go of me and clutched at it. I brought my leg around, snapping my foot on to his wrist. He howled in agony. I lifted off him and kicked the weapon away.

Cassie stood at my side as I got up, glaring at Rivers. 'Now you'll pay for what you did.' Anger flowed out of her, and I knew how she felt. 'We came here for help, and you did this to us.'

A peculiar smile drifted across Rivers's face. Did she expect more of her group to come to her rescue? Behind me, Jenny Blaze was shaking on the floor while her brother cradled his broken bones.

'We collect monsters,' Rivers said. 'And there's no way out of here for the two of you.'

Cassie puffed out her cheeks. 'I'll remove the stake from the vampire and let Bella deal with all of you.'

I shared her annoyance, but was concerned about Cassie's threat. Before I could say anything, something else shocked me even more.

Dr Rivers's legs made an enormous belching sound and shook the chair from side to side. She stood and ripped her trousers off. The flesh from below her waist had disappeared, all of it replaced by shiny metal. One leg kicked Cassie across the room before swivelling to do the same with me. The Dreamcatcher jumped from the girl and fled into the shadows.

Rivers marched towards us. 'Modern technology is such a wonderful thing.'

The cling clang of her legs irritated my ears as the concrete of the wall bit into my shoulders.

Cassie whispered to me, 'She can't move fast with those things. You get around behind while I distract her.' Before I replied, she was on her feet and waving her arms at our metal-limbed attacker, her body concealing my movements. 'This is some amateur rodeo you've been running here.'

Cassie took a step forward. I used her movement to roll to the side and crawl away. The closer steel leg to me twitched, but that was it. I was up and behind Rivers before she noticed what was happening. Her focus was purely on Cassie as I slipped my jacket off.

'The Nexus has been around for centuries before you were born, child, and it will be here for centuries after you're gone. You two may be a riddle we've yet to solve, but the adherents of Dr Dee's work will crack your mystery. That's if I don't crack your heads first.'

Rivers lifted her leg to swing at Cassie's skull, giving me enough time to throw the noose I'd made of my jacket over her metal foot like a cowgirl catching a steer. I pulled back on it as she moved forward, the weight of it and the sudden change of direction taking her down.

She crashed to the floor.

Cassie jumped over the body and grabbed my hand.

'Come on; let's leave before any other goons turn up.'

She dragged me across the room and into the lift. She'd slammed the button to close the door and get us moving before I could say anything. We headed down.

'How do we get out of here?' I said.

'We hit the bottom, head west out of the tunnels, and then we have to go to Whitby.'

'How do you know this?'

'Bella told me.'

We stopped moving and the door slid open. A chill wind whipped around us as we stepped out with no consideration for any potential waiting danger.

I scanned the damp walls and cold concrete. 'And you trust the pretend vampire?'

'I trust her more than those other lunatics, and give your head a shake.' She frowned at me. 'Bella is a real vampire, and monsters exist.'

Cassie pointed to the tunnel to our left, and we ran.

We sprinted for ten minutes, splashing through puddles and scaring the rats away, breathing in the damp and the dust, before finding the steps to the surface. We scrambled up and heaved the cover into the dirt. It was a relief to feel the drizzle on my face and taste nature on my tongue.

'We're near to where we came in,' Cassie said. 'The bike is this way.'

She was off and running before she finished talking. I scampered after her through the mud.

It had been a crazy, illuminating day, and I hoped the bike hadn't been towed away because I hadn't bought a parking ticket.

11 SING ME TO SLEEP

It was daylight when we escaped. The sun filtered into my eyes and a gentle breeze swept the drizzle away and cooled the scars on my face. My bruised eye throbbed. We ran past departing tourists, stabled horses, and an overgrown garden filled with picnickers.

'Thank God,' I said, ignoring the irony and pleased to see the motorbike unscathed and where we'd left it. Cassie handed me the helmet as I gazed behind us, expecting pursuers and finding nothing. I took hold of her fingers.

'Are you okay?' What had happened to her with the Dreamcatcher worried me.

'I'm fine, maybe-sister.' I didn't flinch when she said those words, a warm glow replacing the cold of Dr Rivers and her organisation. 'But you still stink of death. We need to leave here, get cleaned up and go to Whitby.'

'Why go to Whitby? What did Bella tell you?'

She glanced over my shoulder, then back to me.

'You heard what I said when the Dreamcatcher poked into my brain?'

'I did. Was that a genetically modified human?'

She leant away from me and thumped her helmet against the bike, eyes and nostrils flaring.

'You still don't believe in monsters and the supernatural after everything you've seen?'

My mind was exhausted, struggling to find scientific explanations for what I'd witnessed inside the Nexus. There was no explanation for some of it, not yet.

'I'm not sure what I believe anymore, but whatever the Dreamcatcher was, it found the earliest memory of your birth. We have the name of the hospital.'

She clutched the helmet to her chest. 'St Claire's Hospital, but there could be dozens of those across the country. Bella told me to find the Warwitch in Whitby. So that's what I'll do. You can either come with me or stay here.'

Before I could ask what a Warwitch was, she strapped on the helmet and was astride the bike. I slid in behind her.

'I need to go back to my flat first.'

Cassie sighed and turned to me. 'Why?'

'I'll tell you when we get there.' She peered right into me, my mirror image scrutinising the face we shared. 'Otherwise, you can leave me here, and I'll make my own way back.'

'It's that important to you, returning to Middlesbrough?'

I nodded and waited for her to refuse. But she didn't, and we set off as the tide washed over the Lindisfarne Causeway.

Somehow, I managed to relax on the two-hour journey, clinging on to her and thinking of everything I'd witnessed inside the Nexus. My brain continued to insist there were logical reasons for what I'd encountered: Rivers's prisoners were experiments kept hidden from the public. But who controlled the Nexus? Was it the government? I was too young to vote, but this latest bunch had only been in power a few months, led by a charismatic former movie star, Sam Howard. I took little interest in politics, but knew him from the internet and his wide flashing smile. He had a young family and the gift of the gab.

But Rivers said the Nexus was centuries old, and if that was true, it sounded like one of those clandestine organisations you found in James Bond movies or spy novels. And did it even matter who was in charge?

Yes, it did. I thought of Sarda's prison as Cassie broke the speed limit and weaved between lorries big enough to crush us with one false move. Whatever happened on this trip to Whitby, I needed to return to Lindisfarne to free those unfortunates imprisoned and experimented on.

And they must have been experiments. How else could I explain what I'd seen with the Dreamcatcher and Bella? As we sped through the traffic, I even wondered if any of it was real. Perhaps I was still back at my flat, and some of Bob and Terry's hallucinogenic cigarettes had wangled their way into my brain. Maybe they were still alive, and I'd see them again when we got to Middlesbrough.

I hung on to that thought as I clung to Cassie and set the jukebox in my head to a random Tamla Motown playlist. Marvin Gaye sang to me about poison blowing in the north and south, and east as Cassie drove up Linthorpe Road and parked outside Dorman Museum. We got off the bike together and removed our helmets.

'It's best if we walk from here. We don't want to get too close until we know if the police are looking for you or not.'

I didn't argue with her as we hung on to the helmets and strode through the gates of Albert Park.

'Have you always lived in this town?' Cassie said.

I nodded. 'I was shifted around different council estates, lived in several care homes.'

Cassie scanned everything as we went, her eyes twitching everywhere as she spoke.

'That must have been hard for you.'

The sun caressed my face as I shrugged. 'I was different to the other kids in more ways than one. They always seemed to have someone: friends or relatives who couldn't look after them, but still visited. Poverty and deprivation were the norm, environments not the best for encouraging ambition and progression. Most of the other kids seemed resigned to living off handouts and food banks. But ambition burnt inside me, regardless of how much others tried to beat it out of me.'

She stopped walking and stared at me. 'Beat?'

The smell of fresh-cut grass drifted into my lungs as I picked at my past and gave it back to my lookalike.

'Not physically. I got into a few fights early on, but the bullies tend to back down once you fight back. No, it was emotional harassment I suffered from kids and the adults who were supposed to look after me.'

'I'm sorry, Alice. Do you want to talk about it?'

I shook my head. 'Not now, maybe when we're settled somewhere. What I will say is that not everyone was terrible to me.'

'You had at least one friend?'

We started walking again as I remembered the woman who had taught me so much.

'Yes, I suppose so. I was six when I met Ms Peel, and she was more than twenty years older than me, but I like to think of her as my friend.' The thought of her brought a smile to my face as we approached the spot where the werewolf had chased Akemi and me not so long ago.

Akemi: she might have been my first real friend close to my age. I hoped she was okay.

'Was Ms Peel a foster parent for you?'

I glanced across at the lake and remembered those claws going down Akemi's back.

'No. She worked for Artemis and was the one who first brought me to their attention.' I looked at her as we walked. 'So I owe much to her and Artemis for the opportunity to go to university and live independently. That's why I need to see what happened here. I owe it to them, and Bob and Terry, to find answers. And justice.' She nodded and listened. 'What about you, Cassie? Those things you said through the Dreamcatcher sounded traumatic.'

She let out a deep sigh. 'I was shoved from pillar to post across most of the north-east, mainly Sunderland and Newcastle, though there were some brief stops along the coast. Middlesbrough was one of the few places I'd never visited until the other night.' She stared towards the boating lake. 'It's funny how things work out.'

'I'm not laughing.' I didn't want to make this about me. 'What you said through the Dreamcatcher. Was it painful?'

'Do you mean reliving my memories or the fact a super-natural creature had its fingers stuck up my nose and in my brain?'

'Your life growing up, having to deal with those terrible things by yourself.'

Cassie shrugged. 'I guess it wasn't much different from what most young girls go through, fighting off monsters and creeps. What about you?'

'Most people left me alone once I started ignoring them. All my friendships were in books.'

'It sounds lonely.'

I zipped the hoodie right up to my chin. 'I didn't have time for that. I was too busy reading and studying.'

'When did you realise you're a genius?'

My cheeks flushed. 'I wouldn't say I'm a genius. I'm just good at remembering things and working stuff out.'

'These Artemis people must think you're a whizz kid, or they wouldn't have sent you to university at sixteen or got you somewhere to live.'

The thunder of feet hurried past us, childish voices shouting for joy as they headed for the playground, leaving the mothers, sisters, guardians, and nannies in their wake. I watched them go, wondering if I'd ever been that happy as a child and had forgotten about it.

A hint of mint and sweetness hung in the air as a tall woman wearing the tightest jeans spat coffee into the grass and smiled at me before following behind the mass of youthful joy invading the playground.

'Artemis has links with most of the care facilities in Teesside. Sometimes they run competitions for the kids in some of the group homes. I entered one when I was twelve and won.'

'What kind of competition?'

'This was a maths one. The first prize was a new calculator.'

Cassie's laugh was loud enough to scare the birds from the trees around us. They scattered high into the air, flying out of the park, free to travel wherever they wanted.

'I bet they were swamped with excited contestants.'

I ignored her ridicule. 'I didn't do it for the prize since I didn't need a calculator.'

'You must have been popular with the other kids.'

'No, not really.' She had to grin before I understood the sarcasm. 'But it didn't matter. I was testing myself, not looking for approval.'

'And this is how Artemis spotted your talents?'

'I guess so. I'd never given it much thought up to now.

After Ms Peel introduced me to them, it was all go after that as they sent me on classes for kids a lot older than me. Eventually, it led me to university here.'

'And then you bumped into me.'

'That's one way of putting it.'

She touched my arm, and goosebumps sprang up along my skin.

'So why have we come back here, Alice? We need to get to Whitby.' Her smile warmed my heart. 'And I need something to eat and a hot bath. Not necessarily in that order.'

My legs ached as we walked. 'I need to see what happened at the flat. Maybe Bob and Terry survived.'

Cassie grabbed my hand and dragged me into the shadows around the trees.

'They're dead, Alice. You saw what happened to them. And the police might still be here and probably looking for you.'

A chill breeze caressed my face as invisible fingers clutched at my heart. What she said was true, but I'd been ignoring all the evidence of my eyes and hoping everything that had happened to me since the university bar was a hallucination. Wasn't it possible someone had spiked my drink that night, maybe the barman with the dirty hands, and I was still in a dream state? That would explain all the impossible things I'd experienced since. If I marched across this park up to my flat, then the fantasy would come crumbling down.

Cassie let go of me and I gazed at her. If all that had happened in this fantasy world vanished, I'd lose her as well. Would I do that, sacrifice a life with her to go back to what I had? She must have read my mind.

'You think you're in *The Matrix*, don't you?'

'What's that?'

'You've never seen *The Matrix*?' She stared at me as if I thought the Earth was flat. 'It's one of the greatest movies ever.'

'I don't watch films.'

Cassie shook her head, which I found a little bit unnerving. 'The movie is a dystopian future in which humanity is unknowingly trapped inside a simulated reality, the Matrix, which intelligent machines have created to distract humans while using their bodies as an energy source.'

'That actually sounds quite interesting. And plausible.'

'You're damn right it's interesting, my maybe-sister. But what do you mean it's plausible?'

'Well, there's a theory that we could be virtual beings living in a computer simulation. In 2003, the Swedish philosopher Nick Bostrom imagined a technologically adept civilisation with immense computing power that needs a fraction of that power to simulate new realities with conscious beings. And the idea has deep roots in Western and Eastern philosophical traditions, from Plato's cave allegory to Zhuang Zhou's butterfly dream.'

Cassie's bulging eyes made me wonder if I'd ever looked that surprised. 'So, we could just be some lab rats for an alien species somewhere in the universe?'

I smiled at the idea of it. 'It's possible.'

She laughed at me. 'And you think I'm crazy for believing in the supernatural.'

'I never said you were crazy.'

'You didn't need to since it has been in your eyes every time I've mentioned werewolves, or monsters, or demons. And you still looked like that even when the evidence was right in front of you.'

My fingers brushed against hers. 'I'm sorry.'

'Apology accepted. So how do we know we're not living inside a simulation?'

'We don't, so we should make the best of everything while we can.'

A pair of identical dogs ran past us, playfully snapping at each other.

'Do you want to go back to your old life, Alice? It's only two days in the past. You can hand yourself in to the police and explain everything to them using your immaculate science brain.'

'And what will you do?'

'I'm going to Whitby to find the Warwitch, and then discover what happened to my parents.'

'Perhaps they're our parents.'

'Anything's possible, maybe-sister.'

We'd reached the end of the park, and I glanced over the fence to my flat. It was quiet there, with no signs of the police or the authorities. And no evidence of infected residents or the dead walking around.

I watched the kids playing in the park, taking in the aroma of the trees and the flowers, before reaching for Cassie's hand. We headed back to the bike as she sang a song about blue and red pills.

We refuelled outside Middlesbrough using the last of my cash, then stopped at a spot with a mobile café for something to eat. Cassie went to the van to get some grub, making sure my burger was a veggie. We kept our motorbike helmets on in case anyone recognised us.

'How did you pay for this?'

I took the food and a bottle of fizzy pop from her. We moved past the parked cars, climbed over a wooden railing, and headed to the empty picnic tables. Cassie picked up a discarded newspaper from the only bench available.

'I keep a few credit cards for emergencies.'

She couldn't see my eyes narrowing at her. 'And you let me spend all my cash.' She shrugged as heat bellowed off me. 'I can't eat wearing this helmet.'

Cassie grabbed my hand and dragged me across the grass and on to the moors. We found a secluded spot behind some bushes to sit and remove those claustrophobic helmets.

I stuffed half the veggie burger into my mouth. Cassie

unfurled the newspaper and stared at it; the front page focused on the serial killer still on the loose.

'I bet they never catch him.'

'Is there anything about us in the news?'

Cassie scanned through the pages. 'Nope. Perhaps things will die down as they concentrate on the serial killer.'

She flicked through some scaremongering headlines about conflict in Asia, and they made me think of Akemi. I gazed at the word WAR in large capitals, and I remembered why we were going to Whitby.

'What's a Warwitch?'

'Bella didn't say much, only that this person is both a warlock and witch, whatever that means.' Tomato ketchup dripped over her lips.

Apart from the road a few feet away, the Yorkshire Moors surrounded us. A blaze of colour lay across them like a carpet, red, brown and purples shimmering in the heat. The occasional ladybird brought a tiny splash of life as it flitted through the air. I had to fight the temptation to lie down and fall asleep.

'What do you make of what happened with Rivers and her organisation?'

Cassie belched loudly and grinned at me. 'I thought it was a hoot. What does your perfect scientific mind think of everything you saw?'

I stopped eating and flexed some exhaustion from my shoulders. 'A lot of it has a rational explanation, but some doesn't. The Dreamcatcher and what it did to you was bizarre. What did it feel like?'

She placed her drink on the grass, and insects scuttled around the bottle.

'I was there again, for every part: with you and the werewolf in the park, back with the scumbag murdering monster in the shop, and all the rest. And then in that hospital; the smell of it is still inside my head, the sound of that woman's voice.'

Her hands trembled, her face devoid of her usual confidence. I put my refreshments down, wanting to hug her, but also terrified of the prospect.

'The only monsters I'm sure about are Rivers and those siblings. There was something wrong with all three of them.' Disappointment washed through me as I remembered how I'd thought Jenny Blaze was so nice, only to discover she was the opposite.

Cassie picked up her food and took a huge bite. 'I'm not surprised the government wants to control and use the monsters they catch. It's probably been happening for a long time, some secret supernatural war they fight with other countries and with the monsters.'

'Well, it's documented that Hitler and the Nazis were obsessed with the occult. Esoteric mumbo-jumbo played its part in their murderous mania, and it wouldn't surprise me if others followed suit in believing the supernatural exists.'

'But you still don't, maybe-sister?'

The smile on her face stopped me from shouting at her. I finished my burger.

'How will we find this warlock-witch when we get to Whitby?'

Cassie stood and stretched her legs. 'I don't know what a Warwitch even looks like. But we can mingle with the goths there and poke around for clues.'

My eyebrows curled upwards. 'Goths?'

Cassie looked across the wild greenery and flowers on the moors. 'It's Goth Weekend in Whitby. Don't you know what that is?'

I shook my head. 'I know the Visigoths and the Ostrogoths were the two main branches of the East Germanic tribe known as "Goths", and they went to war with the Roman Empire.'

'Jeez, Alice, have you been living under a rock all your life? The Goth Weekend is an annual alternative music festival held in Whitby. Everyone dresses in black and pretends to be vampires or strange Victorians. You've never heard of Bauhaus?'

'Do you mean the German art school or the band?'

She shook her head and laughed at me. 'You're messing with me, right?'

I grinned at her. 'I have extensive knowledge of music since the 1950s. When you're growing up on your own, it's easy to fall into a life where your hobbies are the only thing which matters, but I didn't know there was a festival for Goths near here.'

'Well, now you do, but we can't go there straight away.'

I emptied the bottle of pop down my throat, the sugar creating a buzz in my head. 'Why not?'

She grabbed her nose and pulled a strange face at me. 'Because you stink. We need to get you and those clothes scrubbed before anything else.'

I ignored her jab at me. 'I'm guessing you've got a plan.'

She dumped her rubbish into the bin, and I followed suit.

'There's a country hotel twenty minutes from here. I've stayed there before. They'll launder our clobber, and we can relax.'

We put our helmets on and made our way to the bike. A shower and fresh clothes sounded like Heaven.

'It's a good job you have your dodgy credit cards. Haven't you ever been caught out with them?'

She started the engine. 'No. And nobody has ever

sussed my fake passport either.' She reached into her jacket and showed it to me. It was a perfect replica and added two years on to her actual age. 'So let's not begin now.'

We rode through the moors, the countryside passing us in a blur. Cassie ignored the speed limit, and we reached the hotel in fewer than fifteen minutes. I was ready for sleep when she pulled into the car park.

My eyes sagged as I peered at the building. 'It's impressive.'

'You keep your head covered while I book the room. There's no need for them to see your black eye and cuts and start asking questions.'

I didn't argue with her as she went inside, staring through the helmet at our forthcoming accommodation: a stately rural house in a peaceful setting, the perfect place for me to forget about vampires, shadow people, and treacherous humans with metal legs.

Cassie was out in five minutes.

'I've booked a twin bedroom suite. They'll be up to take our clothes for laundering in ten minutes, so let's get there and order some room service.'

I followed her inside, removing the helmet, but making sure I kept my face to one side and the black eye away from prying eyes. We entered through a church-like doorway, and even though it was the middle of summer, there was a blazing fire burning in reception. We moved through the corridor on the ground floor, turned left, and Cassie found our room. It was huge and looked out over sumptuous gardens. I threw the helmet on to the carpet and slumped across the nearest bed.

'What are we going to wear while they wash our clothes?' I didn't fancy sitting around naked while we waited.

Cassie closed the door. 'There should be dressing gowns in that wardrobe.'

She pointed at the large closet near the window. I opened it and took one for each of us. Cassie checked the bathroom.

'You take a shower first while I go through the menu.' She came out, and I went in. 'Throw your stuff out. The staff should be here for it soon.'

I removed my clothes and did as she said, catching sight of my body in the mirror as I did so. There were two of me in the room, and I didn't enjoy looking at either of them. The cut on my forehead was nearly healed, the bruise on my eye about faded into nothingness. There appeared to be lines on my face that weren't there two days ago. There were unexpected bruises across my arms and legs, plus a significant dent in my side. How many times had I been attacked since my normal, rational life had transformed into this?

I turned the shower on and struggled to get the right temperature.

The heat washed over me, soothing and stinging at the same time. I could have sunk beneath the waves there and then. I pushed the lethargy from my mind and covered my body with strawberry gel. The aroma sparked my senses as I switched off the water and stepped out and into the bathrobe.

I avoided my reflection and returned to the bedroom, finding Cassie fast asleep clutching the menu. I removed it from her fingers and placed it next to the phone charging on the bedside table. Should I ring Artemis to let them know I was okay? My hand lingered over the device, the sound of Cassie's breathing heavy in my ears. I stared at her, my mirror image, my maybe-sister, and knew what she'd say if I did.

They'll trace the call here.

I left it and flopped on to my bed, hoping sleep would come soon, knowing it wouldn't. The earliest doctor's appointment I remembered was when the man of science had prescribed me sleeping pills. I was seven years old. I never took them, slipping the drugs into the side of my mouth and pretending to swallow as a gaggle of adults watched.

My body settled into the bed. The ceiling peered back as I gazed at the ornate lighting, my mind resembling the cracks in the plaster. How much of Dr Rivers and her menagerie was real, and how much a smokescreen? I rationalised most of it, including Bella, the so-called vampire, but the Dreamcatcher stumped me. It had affected Cassie, and I couldn't deny what I'd seen.

I grabbed hold of the TV remote, muted the sound and turned it on. There was an option to add internet access to the bill, and I selected it while Cassie snored. The first thing I did was go through the local news for the last few days. The police had no ID for the boy found in the lake, but were treating it as a murder investigation. There was nothing about Akemi. I scanned social media for her, adding her name to that of the university. She wasn't hard to find on Facebook, but hadn't posted in a week. The last thing she'd liked was a link to a post from the outgoing commander of US forces in the Indo-Pacific region, warning of a Chinese invasion of Taiwan. Perhaps she wasn't joking about working on a nuclear option for her homeland.

The two dead bodies and missing owners of the café garnered little attention apart from a small paragraph on the local newspaper's website. Four months of unpaid rent led to the belief they'd done a runner connected to criminal activities. There was no mention of murderous hairy people.

Next, I searched for any news of what had happened in my block of flats. The police had cordoned off the area and claimed it as a chemical spill, but the internet conspiracy theories were already in overdrive; not claiming it as a zombie attack, but an espionage assignment gone wrong, an assault on British soil, probably by the Russians or the Chinese. I read through some comments before sinking into the pillows.

My mind returned to the events in the cells under Lindisfarne. Was Sarda safe, or did Tom Blaze speak the truth when he claimed to have killed him? I went back on the internet and checked out Rivers's claim for those creatures.

A Glycon was an ancient snake god, the Baba Yaga a supernatural creature from Russian folklore, and the Shadow Person was a modern phenomenon, a spiritual shade from the underworld. The cyclops I was familiar with. I could find a scientific explanation for them all, except the Dreamcatcher. The image of it perplexed my brain as I fell asleep.

***

A KNOCK WOKE me from my slumber. I wiped the haze from my face and lifted my body. Cassie stood, back in her regular clothes, and answered the door to let the refreshments in. She narrowed her eyes as she stared at the member of staff I couldn't see. One hand was on the door, while the other rested on the knife in her pocket. A flash of red stained the top of the blade.

'You're very suspicious,' I said as she brought the tray in and shut the door. She placed the food on the table.

'It's the only way to be.'

I swung my legs around and hopped off the bed. There was a cut on her cheek, which hadn't been there before.

'What happened to your face?'

Cassie removed the knife from her back pocket and placed it next to the tray. My clean clothes lay at the bottom of my bed.

'There was a stray hair I needed to get rid of. We girls need to look our best.' Something was wrong, but I couldn't work out what it was. There were two plates of steak and chips. 'I ordered for you while you slept.'

'Did you forget I'm a vegetarian?'

She blinked her eyes and her fingers wobbled. Behind her were bits of broken glass on the floor, which hadn't been there earlier. She slapped her head and grinned at me.

'Silly me; it slipped my mind.'

She moved her hand towards the knife. I took one plate, a fork, and stepped nearer the bed.

'Who are you?'

She stuck out her lips and threw up her hands, grabbing the blade as she did so.

'What do you mean, sister?'

Not maybe-sister, but sister.

I moved to put the bed between us. 'We're not related.'

Her eyes glazed over. 'You're not, even when you're identical?'

'What have you done to Cassie?'

She shook her head. 'Don't worry, child. I need you both alive, though I don't have to be gentle with you, so you better behave.'

'Where is she?' An aroma of fresh lemon drifted off my clothes.

She held out her knife-less hand and stretched it across the room like that plastic guy from the Fantastic Four. Her elongated fingers disappeared under the bed, returning with Cassie's body, her hands and feet bound, her mouth gagged. Her eyes were about to burst from her head. Her doppelgänger impostor removed the gag, and there were three of me in the room.

Cassie scowled at me. 'Are you deaf? This thing attacks me, then I cut it across the face, and we stumble into furniture and break a glass, and you still don't wake up.'

'I'm an insomniac, but when I fall asleep, I'm out for good. The knock on the door woke me up, though.'

She struggled against her restraints. 'Well, that's great. You must kill this shapeshifter now.'

I clutched the fork and wondered how I'd do that.

13   CEMETERY GATES

'Now, girls, don't make this any harder than it needs to be.' The fake doppelgänger moved towards me. I had a plate of food in one hand and a fork in the other; they were my only weapons.

'What are you?'

'I'm what your sister said, a shapeshifter.'

'She's not my sister, so show your true self.'

A crooked grin crossed her face, across my mirror image, and I wondered if that's how strange it looks when I smile. Her skin rippled like waves rushing towards sand before her head shimmered and fell apart, twisting and changing into a bald man with piercing green eyes. The body followed suit, transforming from female to male in an instant. Even the clothes changed from Cassie's jeans and top to a hotel uniform. There was no way science could explain it. If my mouth had opened any wider, it might have dragged me into the carpet.

The shapeshifter smiled like a politician ready to promise me the world. 'I never reveal my true face at work, but the reward for you two is worth the risk.'

Cassie rolled away from the bed. 'No amount of money will make up for what Alice is about to do to you.'

The shapeshifter sneered at her. 'The bounty on you girls isn't cash.' He rubbed his hands together, and I noticed his skin was still quivering. 'It's much more than that.'

He moved his head from side to side and mumbled some tune I couldn't hear. While he was distracted, I threw the plate at him. The steak bounced off his cheek and sent him sprawling backwards. As he clutched at his face, I was up on the bed and jumping forward. My foot hit his stomach before he could defend himself, and then the strangest thing happened.

'What the?' Cassie shouted as she tried to get free of her restraints.

My leg disappeared into his stomach up to my knee. It was as if I'd jumped into a giant bowl of jelly as I twisted myself to get my elbow up towards his face. But he got momentum before I could, grabbing my arm and rolling us over the carpet and into the far wall.

The concrete hit my hip and sent a surge of electricity running through my bones, but it also shook me loose from his guts. My leg snapped out of him, and I jerked up as he struggled.

He was on the floor as I pushed the fork an inch from his throat. As he begged for mercy, I punched him in the nose. His skin was putty, with no strength to his bones, but at least I didn't lose my fingers inside his flesh. He was out like a light as I pulled my arm back.

'I'm impressed,' Cassie said as I undid the knots binding her.

I rolled him on to his side. 'What shall we do with him?'

She pushed past me and grabbed some chips from the plate.

'I'm starving. I'll eat this steak, you can get cleaned up, and then we'll kill the shifter.'

Bits of him dripped off my leg and on to the carpet.

'No. I'm not killing anyone or anything.' I took the rope and tied his feet and hands together. I added the gag to his mouth. 'Let's leave him and get out of here.'

Cassie emptied a mustard sachet on to the meat and bit into it.

'We can't go yet. It's late, and we need more rest. We can head out to Whitby in the morning.'

'What about him?'

She shrugged. 'If you don't want to kill him, we'll stick him under the bed for the night.'

It didn't sound ideal, but what choice did we have? I went to the table and ate a handful of chips from her plate. She scowled at me.

'Okay, but we should question him first about this bounty.'

Cassie wiped mustard from her lips and knelt next to his head.

'I think he might be out for a while.' She smiled at me. 'You're stronger than I thought.' She put her foot on his body and rolled him in the spot under the bed she'd recently vacated.

'Whoever is looking for you, or the both of us, how did they know we were here?'

'The shifter works here and probably recognised me when we checked in. He brought our clean clothes and jumped me when I let him into the room. I must have been half asleep for him to get the better of me.'

I pointed at her bed. 'You think we'll be safe with him under there?'

She scratched at her chin. 'This isn't the first shifter I've dealt with, but I don't believe he can change into something else to slip out of those ropes. I think they have to taste the blood or flesh of what they want to become, which is why he cut me.' She held up her hand to show me the fresh scar. 'So, as long as he hasn't eaten any small animals in his life, we should be okay.'

The thought of eating made my stomach rumble. I finished her chips and flopped on to my bed.

'I guess supernatural creatures exist then.'

Anxiety clutched at my guts while adrenalin flowed through my veins, one part of my brain fighting with the other.

She chewed on the last of the steak and sat next to me.

'It's about time you came to your senses, maybe-sister.'

I laughed as my bones begged for rest; what little sleep I'd had wasn't enough. My shoulders dropped and I pressed my back into the bed.

'We need to talk about this when we're somewhere safe.'

Cassie hovered over me, smelling of grilled meat and fried chips. She moved a stray hair from my face and stared at me.

'We'll have a conversation in Whitby tomorrow. It won't take long to get there.'

As she finished those words, a veil of sleep descended, and my eyes flickered to a close.

IT WAS eight in the morning when I woke. Cassie was pacing around the room. Fresh eggs and toast were on the table as I climbed out of bed.

'You ordered breakfast?'

She crunched through a piece of brown bread. 'It was part of the package. We need fuel before we go.'

I strode forward, picked up a fork and scooped omelette into my mouth. It was warm and tasted of delicious cheese. The aches had left my body and I felt born again.

'What about our unexpected guest?' I stared at her bed.

'He's awake under there. You know if we leave him alive, he could tell others we were here.' Her eyes flickered with murderous intent.

'Let me get cleaned up and dressed, and I'll tell you my plan.'

I grabbed my gear and went to the bathroom, brushed my teeth using my finger and washed my face, trying to avoid the mirror at all times. I slipped my clothes on and returned to the room. Cassie had pulled the shifter from under the bed. He was propped against the table with fear bursting from his eyes.

I put my shoes on and ignored his gaze.

'What's your plan, Alice?' Cassie appeared to be enjoying herself.

I opened the curtains and gazed out the window. Glorious sunshine had spread its yellow tendrils over the gardens. Even with the windows closed, I smelt the summer outside. I took out my blade, knelt next to the shifter and removed his gag. His lips trembled and saliva dribbled from his mouth. I tilted my head and peered at Cassie.

'She thinks we should kill you, and, all things considered, it might be our only option.' I used the knife to cut his restraints. 'You're a shapeshifter, is that right?'

His face shuddered as he nodded. 'Yes.'

'As a species, are you loners wanting to get away from other shifters because you don't trust being around those who can look like you?'

Illumination sparkled behind his eyes. 'How did you know?'

I took his hand and pulled him up and on to Cassie's bed. I watched her frown at me.

'It's an educated guess. I believe all intelligent thinking creatures follow the same basic patterns. We want love and affection. We fear others, seek sanctuary in isolation, or pursue selfish goals for our satisfaction, regardless of how it affects the world. Life is a constant puzzle we're all trying to figure out.' I sat next to him on the bed. 'Do you know how your death will make things easier for us?'

His shaking returned, his gaze never leaving mine.

'Because then nobody will know you've been here.'

I patted his knee. 'There is that, but my doppelgänger over there believes if we kill you while you look like us, then you'll keep our image, and you realise what that means.'

'Everyone searching for you will think you're dead and they'll cancel the bounty.'

'Excellent.' I took the knife and ran it over my fingers, the cut making my hand flinch. I placed the redness up to his face and moved it across his lips. He couldn't help himself, his tongue twisting out and tasting my blood. 'Now, change into me.'

I got up from the bed and watched the transformation, transfixed again as his head collapsed into a bowl of nothingness before rearranging skin and bone until he was me, including a cut on the forehead and a fading black eye. At that moment, if I hadn't been converted before, I became a true believer in supernatural things.

Cassie moved closer. 'I like this idea, maybe-sister.'

My focus was on my new doppelgänger. 'Do you think you're in danger from me?'

Tears formed in the shifter's eyes and I tried not to let

the sight bother me. To the best of my knowledge, I'd never cried in my life.

'Yes,' she sobbed.

I placed my hand on her shoulder. 'Good, but I promise to spare you if you do as I ask. Do you understand?'

The shifter never hesitated. 'Yes.'

I smiled, enjoying the confused look on Cassie's face.

'This is what I want you to do.'

TEN MINUTES LATER, we were out of the hotel and on the road. Another twenty after that, and we were in the seaside town of Whitby and eyeing up the ice-cream sellers. There was a lack of people dressed as goths creeping around, and I only found out later that Cassie had got the dates wrong for the festival.

She slurped on a strawberry cone with a flake sticking from the top of it.

'You trust the shifter to do what you asked?'

I drank from a bottle of fizzy pop, the orange flavour cooling my mouth in the summer heat.

'It was leave the hotel and head in the opposite direction while looking like me, or you'd slit his throat. So yes, I think he's too scared to do anything else.' I held my hand over my face to shield my eyes from the sun. 'So, how are we going to locate this mysterious Warwitch?'

Cassie finished her cone and removed her jacket. She'd parked the bike opposite, paying for a ticket this time. There was no telling how long we'd need to be there, and I was thinking about somewhere to stay.

'To find this Warwitch, we stick to my tried and trusted routine. The supernatural is always connected to spiritual things, so we visit the oldest church in town and mooch around there.'

I'd watched a documentary before about Whitby and knew it could only be one place. I pointed over the water at the ancient stones atop the cliffs.

'We should start there then.'

Cassie had her phone out, checking the information on Wikipedia. 'The Church of Saint Mary: A Norman church built on the site around 1110, added to and altered over the centuries. The tower and transepts are from the 12th and 13th centuries. The church graveyard is a setting in Bram Stoker's novel, *Dracula*.'

I wiped the dust from my trousers as I stood. 'Well, that seems fitting.'

Cassie flicked her fingers across the screen. 'What about Whitby Abbey? It's the ruins of a 7th-century Christian monastery.'

'We can check them both, but we might as well start with the church since it's the closer.'

And it meant climbing up the cliffs. As more tourists descended upon the town, we made our way to the flight of steps that would take us up. Kids flocked around the places selling candy and glittering trinkets while the adults queued outside the fish and chip shops or loitered in the doorways of the pubs, probably hoping the alcohol would cool them from the blaze of the sun.

The streets were cobbled and hurt my feet as I struggled to keep up with Cassie. She seemed to be in a hurry, perhaps doubting I'd talked the shifter into doing what I wanted.

'I'm glad you've accepted the truth of things.' Cassie didn't look at me as we walked. 'It must put a strain on that science brain of yours.' She appeared to enjoy teasing me.

I dodged a ferocious-looking dog that had slipped from its lead. I considered her comment.

'Any sufficiently advanced technology is indistinguishable from magic.'

She stopped walking and scrunched her eyes at me. 'Are those your words?' Next to her was a shop selling vampire caps, plastic fangs and bottles of "real" blood.

'It's a quote from Arthur C Clarke. I believe what we call the supernatural exists, but there'll be scientific reasoning behind what I've seen with further exploration. It's the main purpose I'm following you on this quest.'

The laugh came from her eyes first, her pupils sparkling and springing large before it erupted from her mouth and made her nose twitch. She put her arm on my shoulder, her joy running through her body and transferring to me as a movement of uncontrollable sinew pushing up against unmovable bone.

'Oh, maybe-sister, what am I going to do with you?'

Before I could reply, she was moving again: a giant, loping stride as if she was hunting something. I followed, striding by the candy floss stalls and towards the mackerel shop at the base of the famed one hundred and ninety-nine steps.

We moved past houses on either side, stepping beyond kids trying to run up the steps and blokes sticking out their chests as if the climb was a test of their masculinity. The harbour was behind us, a flock of seagulls above. A quarter of the way there, Cassie and I were side-by-side, with determination written across her face in stone. The chaos which had engulfed me over the last few days was what she'd lived with for two years. I couldn't fathom how difficult it must have been for her. I'd grown accustomed to my isolation, took comfort in my solitary life, but it can't have been easy for her to be on her own to deal with the things I'd seen since going into the park.

Halfway there and the landscape opened up right and left, the climb getting steeper, the tourists thinning out as they struggled to breathe. Cassie strode on, never missing a step, appearing to get stronger the closer we got to the top. It was as if there was a magnet up there, pulling me in. Something felt different in the air. I tilted my head, expecting static and lightning to appear from the clouds, only finding birds circling above.

I stopped to ease the pressure on my lungs, turning to gaze over the town below. The view was breathtaking, the coast and countryside separated by the picturesque sprawl of the buildings. Cassie didn't pause and kept going. I sucked in my chest, flexed my legs and continued. A cool breeze settled on the sweat on my head, my fingers gripping the railing at my side. The metal was old and rusted, life coming away from it in bits. The aroma of the sea was everywhere.

When I reached the top, Cassie was sitting on a bench with a large cemetery behind her. I was at the point where I could have fallen into an open grave and rested for a while. Instead, I flopped next to her.

I coughed loudly enough to scare the birds gathering around us.

'I think my chest will burst.'

She handed me a tissue for the sweat cascading down my forehead.

'I thought you'd be fitter than this, maybe-sister.'

I wiped at my face and struggled to smile. 'I'll beat you next time.'

As more tourists reached the top, I noticed the occasional stare in our direction. Was the sight of two girls who looked exactly alike that unusual? I wondered what these people would think if a Glycon confronted them or a Dreamcatcher, not to mention an encounter with a shapeshifter. Deep down, what did I think of them, and all the others?

Cassie gazed across the tombstones, towards the church and the abbey beyond.

'Did you feel the energy as we walked up? I imagined we'd be struck by lightning at any second.' She twisted her head upwards. 'And what's with all these birds flapping around us? It's like we're in a Hitchcock movie.'

I was about to explain to her how static electricity builds up in the air and its effect on animals, but thought better of it. We were on the supernatural path for now.

'If I live and breathe, and I surely do, it's the Whitby Doppelgängers here before me.'

I looked up to see a man standing opposite. The first thing I noticed was his eyes, a deep brown which shimmered and melted into the colour of his face. He had the long hair of a 1970s rock star and the clothes of someone about to attend their funeral. He clutched an ornate wooden walking stick, topped off by a snake's skull. I imagined him smashing guitars, trashing hotel rooms while pursuing wild women and Byzantine drug problems.

A sudden pain gripped my chest. 'What did you say?'

He didn't move from his spot, resting his backside on the gravestone behind him. When he opened his mouth, a flash of gold shimmered from half his teeth.

'Local folklore tells of a visitor to the town who bumped into his doppelgänger. You may think this is of no consequence, but it has been known for doppelgängers to steal the immortal soul of their lookalike. The only way to prevent this is to challenge the doppelgänger to reveal their true self before they can rest a finger on you. Doppelgängers hate violence, so they soon scuttle away with their tails between their legs.'

'What happened in the folk tale?' Cassie said.

'Why,' the man said, 'I got to him before he could speak, and so I live to tell the tale. Now you have to ask yourselves, am I the visitor or the doppelgänger?'

Seagulls swirled and squawked everywhere, something cracked in the sky, but there was no sign of thunder or lightning. Cassie was up with a knife in her hand as I pulled her back.

I peered deep into his face. 'Are you the Warwitch?'

He held out the cane, tipped an imaginary hat towards us and bowed.

'My name is Kai and I'm at your service, ladies.'

'How did you know we were here?'

'Nothing unusual gets into this town without my knowledge, and I felt your energy the minute you arrived. All I had to do was wait for you to climb up here. Now, if you'd care to follow me.' He turned his back and headed between the graves and into the cemetery.

Cassie and I stared at each other. What other choice did we have? We strode behind him for twenty yards before he disappeared.

And then, so did we.

My feet moved from grass to stone, the surrounding air changing from outside to inside, the light going from natural to artificial. Cassie was at my side, the Warwitch a few yards ahead. We stood on steps, but nothing like we'd climbed to get to the church, for this was an M C Escher illustration made real. One set of steps headed left where it met a corridor, and at the end was an identical set heading down into a sheer gravity-defying drop. Striding up it and refusing to fall was a large white cat. It stared at me through milky green eyes.

Kai was next to me before I realised it. 'Ignore Rufus; he's only showing off. Keep following me.'

He walked up the steps as if on the Moon, feet sticking to the concrete when his body should have dropped into space below. I'd never been afraid of heights, but this was bizarre. My brain told me to stay put as I glanced down to areas filled with books and magazines as if everything was one gigantic library.

Cassie stuck to the wall, face transfixed by what

appeared to be the Warwitch defying the laws of nature. I took hold of her arm.

'Remember, this is the supernatural.'

I smiled and made the first move, sticking my foot up and out, placing it on the step and striding up and after Kai. Rufus peered at me from the other side.

'Okay, you need to give me a scientific explanation for this,' Cassie said as she followed me with her eyes half-closed. I was surprised at how she trembled as we moved, her fingers flicking against mine.

I tried my best to calm her. 'It's all about perception. Wherever we've stepped into, this is an altered landscape. There's no up or down, even though our senses imply otherwise.'

She hesitated in her movement, but I pulled her up. Were we moving up or not? If we were, we should have tumbled to the ground by now. Noises below my feet distracted me from those thoughts. When I looked down, I wished I hadn't. Between the breaks in the steps, human-faced centipedes crawled through the architectural phantasmagoria, scrutinising us.

'Keep walking,' the Warwitch said, and we did. 'If you fall through the gaps, there's no coming back.' It was the first time I'd seen fear on Cassie's face.

I gripped her hand and dragged her next to me. 'I won't let go.'

Her eyes were like pinpricks shrinking into her skin. 'What's that smell?'

I caught a whiff of what she meant: pepper, garlic and fried tomatoes. It was delicious and made me forget for a second about the things which scampered below. I lost my concentration enough to bump into Kai standing at the head of the stairs.

'We've got to hurry, or my Bolognese will burn. I hope you girls are hungry.'

He disappeared over the horizon, and I was convinced he'd fallen down the other side. I stepped over the top and pulled Cassie with me.

'Damn!' I said as we walked into a kitchen. The ground was level and my senses relaxed into normality.

Kai stood over a pan and licked his lips. He winked at me.

'Don't worry. I made it with veggie meat.'

I didn't ask how he knew what I liked as I stared at the paintings of jesters and knaves on the walls, every one of which moved like a living animation. Cassie pulled from my grasp and towards our host, her hand close to where she kept her knives.

'What is this place?'

He had a ladle in his fingers. 'Are you ready for food?'

'Answer the question.'

'That's all in good time, Cassandra Kane.' He scooped some sauce into a bowl and placed it on the table in the middle of the kitchen. A speedy white furball jumped up and lapped at the grub. I gazed at the cat in admiration. 'Rufus refuses to eat from the floor; he says it's barbaric.'

The animal eyed me suspiciously as I stepped further into the room.

'Your cat can talk?'

Kai put more sauce into a bowl and handed it to me. It smelt like the food of the gods.

'Only to me.'

'You'll answer my question now.' Cassie had a knife in her hand and Rufus growled at her.

Kai served himself and sat at the table. I joined him on the other side, ensuring not to get too close to Rufus and those dangerous looking claws. The moggy ignored us and continued to eat. I didn't blame him, as the aroma drew me in like a magnet.

Cassie's face crumpled into a mop of strangled lines, changing her complexion into something resembling a volcano ready to erupt. The Warwitch downed a spoonful of his cooking and turned to my maybe-sister.

'This is the Impossible Palace, a place existing in many dimensions all at the same time. To get in and out safely, you need to find the right entrance and exit.'

I spoke with sauce warming my mouth. 'And what happens if you don't?'

'Do you remember the things you saw scuttling under the steps as you journeyed here?'

The inhuman eyes inside human heads perched on insect bodies were something I wouldn't forget in a while.

'It's hard not to.'

'Well, they'd suck out your brains in an instant given half a chance, and they'd be the least of your worries if you went through one of the wrong doors in here.'

Cassie put the blade down. 'Did you build this place?'

Kai spat food on to the table and made Rufus haunch his back and cringe.

'No, my young friend. I'm only the current guardian of the treasures between its impossible walls.'

It was my turn to recoil on hearing this, his words reminding me of what Ellen Rivers said to us in her underground dwelling. I pushed the bowl away.

'Have you heard of the Nexus?'

He produced a napkin from somewhere and dabbed at his lips.

'Those government people who like to collect things

more special than they'll ever be? Yes, I'm aware of them. Is that why you're here?'

'One of their prisoners told us to search for the Warwitch in Whitby.' I glanced at Cassie. 'We need to know what happened when we were born.'

Rufus jumped into Kai's lap, and the two of them appeared to purr in harmony.

'Can't you find this information online? I have free Wi-Fi here.'

Cassie placed her hands on the table, fingers gripping into the wood.

'We were abandoned at birth. There are no records of our parents, no documents detailing our families or ancestry. We might look like each other, but we don't know if we're related. All we have to go on is the name of the hospital where I was born sixteen years ago.'

I watched her take a deep breath, feeling her frustration but wanting to stay in control. I changed the subject.

'Why are you called a Warwitch?'

Kai got up from the table, clutching the cat.

'I'm a warlock and a witch. What you observe now is my male persona.' He smiled at me. 'Do you wish to see my female half?'

Cassie and I stared at each other, and our eyes grew wide.

'Absolutely,' I said.

As Kai held Rufus, his face trembled, flesh rippling like liquid until it shimmered and changed from masculine to feminine, his broad nose transforming into a thin snout. His brown eyes became her blue ones, his long dark hair turning into her short red locks. He had hands designed to dig trenches, but hers were created to caress piano keys. This was a different process to what I'd witnessed with the shapeshifter.

'What are you?' Cassie said.

The female Kai had a much warmer smile than her male half, lips full and teeth brilliantly white. She dropped Rufus to the floor and held out her hands.

'I am what I am; nothing more, nothing less. One whole made of two parts.'

'If you use magic, can you help us?'

She pondered the question for a few seconds. 'You need to undertake a difficult journey and travel into your past to discover the truth about yourselves.'

Excitement gripped my bones. 'You'll cast a spell to send us back in time?'

The laughter rippled from her like tiny stones skipping across a river.

'Spells and incantations are falsehoods created by men to bind women. All creatures of the many worlds search out power in the wrong way.'

'What do you mean by the wrong way?'

Kai moved around the table and towards a bottle of dark liquid near where she had cooked the food. She picked it up and grabbed three small glasses in her other hand. She wore the same clothes as he, but there was a visible change in Kai's body shape: more slender in form, lighter. She put the glasses on the table and poured out three measures from the bottle. It smelt of the sweetest cherries.

'Some think power comes from binding others to their will. Not only a physical binding, but also mentally, emotionally and spiritually. The greatest way of achieving this is through language. Words are used to bind by the swearing of oaths and promises by signing contracts and deeds, but when words are used against these beings, they will lie, deceive, or manipulate. They claimed the words of women to be witchcraft, that they were using spells against them. So they bound and burnt. Power comes from artefacts and objects. And that's what you need to collect to visit the place and time of your birth.'

Cassie took one glass and sniffed at the liquid before drinking half.

'Okay; I've never encountered either a warlock or witch before, but I believe you. What do we have to do?'

'You must acquire four objects: the Mirror of Time, the Eye of Medusa, an angel's wings and the blood of a demon. You need these to see, to travel, to hold and to control. You'll start with the Mirror of Time because it's the closest object. You'll get it from the collection of the most powerful vampire.'

I picked up one glass and sipped at it, surprised it wasn't alcoholic.

'I've barely accepted that supernatural things exist, and now you're telling me angels are real, and Medusa?'

'All the creatures of your nightmares and beyond exist, Alice. The sooner you accept this, the better it will be for all of us.'

'How do you know our names?' I finished the rest of the drink.

'There is a bounty on your heads, though it was originally only for one of you, and your names seep through the supernatural ether.'

'I've met a vampire called Bella, but when you say the most powerful vampire, you must mean...?'

Cassie couldn't say it, so I guessed. 'You mean Dracula, the first of the vampires.'

Kai picked up the bowls and dropped them to the floor,

only they never reached the ground, disappearing into empty air before they broke.

'Dracula is not the first of the vampires, a name lost to antiquity, but he is Lord of the Undead.'

'Do we have to go to Transylvania?'

'No, Alice. Dracula has long abandoned his ancestral residence in the Carpathians. His spiritual home is in Whitby.'

'Stoker's book was true?'

'All writers tell the truth in their own way. Creative people are closer to the Divine than the rest of humanity. Their worlds and characters exist somewhere, even if it isn't in this reality. In another realm, we three are figments of someone's imagination.'

'Where in Whitby is Dracula?'

'He sleeps surrounded by his most devoted acolytes.'

'He's sleeping?'

'Fame got to be a burden for him about fifty years ago. It started with Stoker's book, but once the movies took off, he was swamped by humans who either wanted to kill him or be converted, not to mention the other vampires who challenged his rule or subjugated themselves at his feet. I think in the early 70s, the stress was too much for him. His therapist told him to rest, so now he sleeps the long sleep of the Undead.'

'Dracula had a psychiatrist?'

'Do you know that TV show *The Sopranos*? That was based on Dracula. The writers just switched it from vampires to the mafia to make it more palatable to an unsuspecting public.'

'If he's been sleeping for fifty-odd years, at least he didn't have to suffer through *Twilight* like the rest of us. I hated those movies.' Cassie was taking this less seriously than I expected.

I focused on what Kai had said about gathering four objects.

'What is the Mirror of Time?'

'It's exactly what it says it is. A mirror you peer into and locate any point in the past. The original vampire created it as a way of connecting to those lost to the ravages of time. Can you imagine what it's like to be immortal and lose everyone around you?'

'So we need this magic mirror to see our birth?'

'Yes. Once you find the point in time, you must journey to it, and the only creatures capable of time travel are angels. Which is why you require a feather from an angel's wings.'

'What's the demon blood for?'

'That's to control time when you get there. Without it, you'll be whisked off to any moment in time. Once you locate your birth in the Mirror of Time, the Eye of Medusa will freeze it so you can use the angel feather to travel there.'

It sounded like the strangest heist in history. 'If Dracula is in Whitby, where are the others?' I didn't even want to ask about angels, not yet.

'Medusa is on the island of Sarpadone near Greece.'

'Do we have to pluck out one of her eyes?'

'No. You have to cut a snake from her head. This will freeze the point in the Mirror of Time. You must do this without looking at the snakes. Otherwise, they'll turn you into a statue.'

Cassie shook her head. 'That's great. And if we survive Dracula and Medusa, it's just an angel and demon we'll need to charm to get what we want.'

Kai bathed us in another of her warm smiles. 'You're in

luck because there's an angel and demon that live together in Hollywood; two birds with one stone.'

I raised my eyebrows. 'My knowledge of celebrities is limited.' And I was struggling to accept angels were real.

'You must have heard of Joy Canto and her husband Patrick Snow, probably the most famous acting husband and wife team since Brad and Angelina.'

'Why would an angel and a demon want to be actors?'

Cassie laughed. 'Because they want fame, wealth, power and sex, why else?'

'Those are human desires. Celestials want something more than that. Angels require devotion and admiration, while the demons seek subjugation and where better to get that than Hollywood? Then, like all Celestials, they feast on human souls.'

'What do you mean when you say Celestials?' My brain buzzed with all the information.

'Celestials are creatures of God.'

'I'm not religious, but according to the Bible, aren't we all creatures of God?'

'What do you know of the Bible and the story of Creation?'

Cassie shook her head. 'I never paid much attention to fairy tales.'

I thought it was a strange thing to say, considering what she'd told me of the supernatural. But I'd read the Bible many times in my trips across orphanages and care homes.

'According to the Bible, God created man in his image.'

Kai grinned. 'And what about women?'

'Created from a useless rib Adam didn't need. I remember that bit,' Cassie said.

'Does that sound like the design work of an omnipotent being to you? Imagine building a house, then realising you have to take out the foundations to add another room. It's more lies and distortions used to bind others. Humanity was created in God's image. Celestials were created from God's flesh. Therefore they all have some supernatural ability because they're closer to the Divine.'

'I'm confused. How can men and women have been created in God's image?' I was trying to find a rational reason for the irrational.

'Think about it.'

I had been thinking about it. 'Are you saying God is both male and female?'

'Bingo,' the Warwitch said and snapped her fingers.

Cassie pulled a face. 'How is that possible?'

'In the beginning, there was nothing but God spending eternity in darkness.' The Warwitch turned to Cassie. 'You've been alone for sixteen years; how lonely have you been?'

Cassie stuck out her lips. 'I don't have time to get lonely. I'm too busy fighting adults, other kids and supernatural monsters to think about being alone.' Her eyes were defiant, but I saw the truth hidden behind them.

'And what about you, Alice?'

I hesitated to speak, reluctant to unburden myself of what I'd held inside me all this time. But then something made me talk.

'You don't have to be alone to be lonely. For as long as I can remember, other people have surrounded me, and I've been lonely all that time. I've learnt to live with it, to use my isolation as a comfort blanket. Loneliness is all I know.'

Silence engulfed the room. Cassie trembled a little.

Kai continued. 'Imagine then what it was like for God to exist in eternal darkness all alone. Imagine, if you can, the depths of that isolation, the extremes of that loneliness. At some point, the Creator created other beings. Men and women were the first of God's creations because God is both male and female.'

'Oh my God,' Cassie said with no irony. 'God has two genders?'

I shook my head at my maybe-sister. 'Gender is a human construction designed to put males and females into restrictive models of behaviour. What the Warwitch is claiming is that God's form comprises both male and female physiology.'

'Oh, wow. I'm not saying I believe all this angels and God stuff, but can you imagine what would happen if God came back to Earth and revealed this to people?'

As a scientist, I didn't believe any of this, but I had an inkling of how traumatic it would be to most of the population.

'It would be the top trending topic on social media.'

Cassie ran with the idea. 'Okay, God made men and women in their image because God is both male and female, but that still doesn't explain what Celestials are.'

'Humanity reflects God; God created humans from their image. Celestials, all supernatural creatures, are of the body of God.'

Kai let us think about it. Cassie blurted it out first.

'You're saying God had sex with - I can't say himself; with themselves?'

'God split into separate male and female parts. The Greeks and all the other religions that mention powerful beings birthed from the gods were near the truth.'

I slumped into a chair, struggling to believe what I'd heard. What was the point of pursuing science if all of this was true?

The Warwitch must have read my mind.

'Remember, Alice: magic is just science waiting to be explained.'

I stared at her. 'How do you know all this?'

'I know because I'm a seer. I can peer into any living creature and see their past and future. It allows one to gain an abundance of knowledge.'

'You can do this with every human and Celestial?' An idea sprang to mind.

'I can; with everyone but you two.'

Then the idea vanished as quickly as it came.

And my head buzzed like drunken bees stuck in a honey jar.

'What?' Cassie's voice rose a notch.

'When I peer into the both of you, something blocks me. All I see is darkness. I don't know what you are.'

Cassie dropped into the seat next to me. 'I need a lie-down.'

I focused on the practicalities of what we had to do. 'Okay, let's say we get this Mirror of Time away from Dracula; how are we going to get to an island near Greece, and then to Hollywood.'

'Remember I told you we don't use spells, but objects?'

I nodded. The Warwitch reached into her jacket and removed a beautifully ornate knife studded with jewels.

'This is the Blade of Reality. It cuts through distance. This will take you to the other side of the world.'

'Can we use it to get into Dracula's lair?' I asked, more in hope than expectation. I didn't think any of this would be easy.

'No. The Blade can't cut into space where the Mirror of Time sits. You must travel there the old-fashioned way.'

'You mean a break-in?' Cassie couldn't hide the excitement in her voice.

'It shouldn't be too hard.' Kai bent to give Rufus a snack. 'He'll be sleeping, so there'll be only the guards to deal with.'

I knew it wouldn't be as easy as she made out. 'What type of security?'

She picked up the cat and he scowled at me.

'There will be some of his human acolytes, maybe a few vampires.'

'And you think we're capable of dealing with that?' I tried to keep the caution out of my voice, but I didn't think it worked by the look on Kai's face.

'You're right,' she said. 'Perhaps you should stay with me and train for a while.'

Cassie slammed her fist into the table. 'No, I can't wait any longer to find out what happened to my mother.' She glanced at me. 'Alice might not care about her past, but I need to know why my parents gave me up.'

I glared at her. 'That's not true, but maybe Kai is right and we should prepare for this meeting with Dracula.'

'Definitely not.' Steam simmered out of Cassie's ears. 'I'll go without you if I have to.'

'You two remind me of the Mermaids of Staithes.'

'What?' Cassie said.

I smiled at her, hoping it would calm her down.

'Staithes is a fishing village a few miles from here. Mermaids are mythical sea creatures.'

My words had the opposite effect on her as her eyes bulged.

'I know those things, Alice. I'm not an idiot.'

Kai stepped in before things got more heated.

'The mermaids took a risk when visiting a human

community. Long before Staithes was a fishing village and popular tourist spot, a terrible storm hit the coast, one that forced the residents away from the water while it raged around them. There's no record of how long the storm lasted, but it must have been for hours as once the people left the safety of their homes, they found many boats damaged and broken. But that wasn't the only thing the shocked villagers discovered.

'As they walked along the beach, picking their way through the debris washed up on the sand, among the piles of seaweed, small crabs and twitching fish was a sight none of them had witnessed before. Two mermaids lay exhausted on the rocks, bruised and sleeping in sight of the houses of Staithes.'

Cassie snorted at Kai. 'Mermaids. I know monsters exist, but that's just silly, a story for kids and little girls who love Disney movies.'

I had to agree. 'Myths and legends continue to fascinate many people, and mermaids are one of the most popular.'

'I guess I'll have to prove it to you.' Before I could move, Kai placed her hands on Cassie and me, and everything went dark.

The light reappeared immediately, but we weren't in Whitby anymore.

And I didn't have any legs.

'What the?' Cassie said as I stared at her, gazing at the green scales that had replaced her legs.

Then I ran my fingers below my waist, watching as the water stuck to my skin, amazed at how much the scales glistened in the sun. The wind whistled around me, and the only thing I heard was the furious beating of my heart against my chest. Then I removed my hand and held it up to the sun.

'Kai did this. To make us understand what happened to the mermaids, she put us in their place.'

Cassie threw her arms in the air. 'I don't care why the Warwitch did this, but how the hell do we move without legs?'

I told my brain nothing had changed and expected my new lower torso to move, but nothing happened: there was no feeling there, no twitching or spasm to indicate that above my hip was connected to what was now below. As I continued trying, Cassie rolled off her rock and hit the sand.

'Are you okay?' I said.

'I'm going to make Kai suffer for this when we get back.' She dug her fingers into the sand and dragged herself towards me.

I looked towards the shadows approaching us. 'That's if we get back.'

Cassie pushed up on her elbows as her flipper, if that's what it was, quivered in the sun. She gazed at the villagers as they approached open-mouthed.

'Can you help us?'

There were about two dozen of them, mainly men, all carrying pikes and pitchforks. The only thing missing was the torches.

But they had nets.

Large fishing nets glistening in the light. And they threw them over us, the material sticking to my arms and head. The men pulled on them, and the nets cut into my skin and scales.

Yes, I could feel those now as they drew blood from me.

'Let me go,' I shouted as Cassie swore at them.

'I'll kill you all when I get out of here.' There was no fear in her eyes, only anger and frustration.

The villagers were silent, with grim determination

drawn across their faces. They pulled on the nets and dragged us across the beach. The sea drifted up to my nose as sand settled on my lungs. Cassie continued to rage against our captors as I coughed my guts up.

They towed us off the sand and up concrete steps, pulling me over sharp stones as I fought to find my breath. The men hauled us up and hung Cassie and me from large wooden poles overlooking the houses. Children scampered out of their homes and gawked at us as we swayed in the wind. The bravest of them came forward to touch our scales, and I felt their pawing fingers grabbing at me.

Women dragged the youngest kids away, but the older ones stayed, picking up stones and approaching us. Cassie shouted at them, but I knew it was futile to protest.

The first stone hit me on the shoulder, sending rippling pain down the whole of my arm. The next landed in my gut, followed by others to my face and head as if someone had dropped me in a cement mixer, crushed up against jagged pebbles, and then spun it at a thousand miles an hour. Strangely, they aimed no stones at my new scales. Perhaps the sight of what made a mermaid unique scared them too much even to throw bricks at my lower half.

'We mean you no harm,' I cried through the pain. 'The storm washed us here, but we want to be in the sea.' The words came from my mouth, but they were not mine; a long-forgotten plea from down the ages.

I asked for help while Cassie raged at our captors, but none of it made any difference. The barrage of stones continued for two minutes until the adults stopped their children, but there was no respite from the abuse. Next, we were prodded and poked with poles and sticks by the men while the women hurled insults at us. We were the Devil's children, demon girls of the sea sent to the village to tempt the fishermen to their deaths on the rocks.

It went on all night until sleep overcame me.

WHEN I WOKE, I expected to be back in Whitby. Instead, I was still hanging from the pole, and what had once been my legs throbbed with pain. I must have swallowed half the beach during the night as my throat was drier than a sandbox, and there was a yawning hole inside my stomach.

'Why are we still here, Alice?'

I twisted my head to look at Cassie. 'I don't know. Maybe Kai didn't mean it to go on as long as this.'

Cassie gurgled, but the next words I heard came from below me.

'Are you creatures thirsty?'

I glanced down at the young woman. She couldn't have been more than five or six years older than us, and I peered into her dark brown eyes.

'We're human, just like you.'

She shook her head, but offered me a cup of water. I drank it as if it was the last water on earth, gulping greedily until I nearly choked. Then she refilled the cup and did the same with Cassie.

'It's terrible what they've done to you, but you're no more people than the goats in the yard. You're not the demons of the sea the others claim, but you're something different, sirens or mermaids.' She glanced over her shoulder, and I guessed she was fearful the others would see her kindness and assume it was weakness. 'You're different, and we don't like different around here. Why, it was only last week a traveller came to the village and told us the tale of the Frenchman washed ashore at Hartlepool who was all covered in hair and spoke a terrible language like an animal.'

I licked the water from my top lip. 'And they hanged him, didn't they?'

She nodded. 'Yes, and I fear the same fate awaits both of you.'

'You could let us down,' Cassie said.

'No.' She shook her head and turned to leave. 'I can afford you this small mercy, but if I release you, then your fate will befall me. You should have stayed in the sea with your own kind.'

And with that, she left, and I saw the children with their stones gathering in the distance.

'I'm going to kill Kai for this,' Cassie said.

I gritted my teeth, closed my eyes and waited for the first hit.

But it didn't come, and when I opened my eyes, we were back in Whitby, sitting opposite the Warwitch.

Cassie growled and threw herself at Kai. I readied my aching bones to stop their fight, amazed to see Cassie bounce off an invisible barrier and fall at my feet.

'It was important for you to experience adversity before setting off on your quest to discover your beginnings. For if you can't deal with a little suffering, how will you handle the danger of Dracula and the other tasks ahead of you?'

Cassie picked herself up and cracked her knuckles. 'How did you do that?'

Kai tapped the side of her head. 'I have a wealth of history inside here, and as the guardian of this magnificent place, I can transfer the living experiences of the past to others. It's better than virtual reality, don't you think?'

I placed my hands on my legs and remembered the scales I'd had.

'What happened to the mermaids?'

Kai let out a deep sigh. 'The villagers imprisoned them for months, so long they got used to their strange appearance, and people even began talking to them. Nobody was shocked to see them anymore, so the stone-throwing and abuse stopped. One day, the mermaids managed to charm a young man into letting them free for a moment. They convinced him to take them to the beach, knowing when the tide was due, and tricked him into leaving them for a second to get them something to eat. Once he left, they used the waves to swim out to sea. And they were never seen again by the villagers of Staithes.'

'Fantastic.' Cassie flopped into the sofa. 'Are you going to play any more mind games, or can we go and get what we need from Dracula?'

Kai stared at us both. 'I guess it's now or never.'

I rubbed at my legs and remembered the sea.

16 THE HOUSE OF THE RISING SUN

assie clapped her hands together in anticipation. 'Let's move then. The sooner we get there, the quicker we'll have what we need. Do you know where he lives?'

Kai stuck her fingers behind the cat's ear and brought out a piece of paper. She handed it to me.

'I wouldn't call it living.'

'He's at St Hilda's Terrace. Is that far from here?'

'It's a fifteen-minute walk down into town and across the river.'

Cassie took the address from me. 'Can't we use the Blade of Reality to cut our way to outside the house?'

Kai shook her head. 'I won't let the Blade anywhere near Dracula, sleeping or not.' She walked towards the large fridge at the back of the kitchen. 'Follow me, and I'll show you the safe way out.'

Cassie slipped the paper into her trouser pocket as we strode behind Kai. The Warwitch opened the fridge and I assumed she was still hungry. Light blazed out, but not from a regular fridge because St Mary's Church cemetery was on the other side. Cassie and I stepped through the gap, finding we were only a few feet away from where we'd entered the Impossible Palace. A group of kids stared at us in bemusement.

I turned to speak to Kai.

'What will you do while we try to get this mirror?'

'I'll be looking after Rufus.' With that, she closed the door, and normality reigned above the town of Whitby.

'If we're going up against vamps, we have to be prepared.'

Cassie strode towards a group of trees. I followed her.

'Prepared, how?' I glanced at the church. 'Do we need holy water and garlic?'

'Garlic is useless against vamps. I've never tried holy water, but I doubt it would be any better.' She picked up two broken branches. 'I'm not an atheist like you because I've encountered too many strange things to disregard anything, but even though I've fought demons, I'm having a hard time believing in angels and God. What about you?'

She handed me a branch.

'It's all about evolution.'

Cassie removed her knife and started sharpening the end of the wood. I did the same.

'Are you still looking for a scientific rationale for this? I thought you'd given up on that.'

I sat on the ground and she joined me, pushing clumps of leaves to the side. Under the bright summer sky, a heaving, surging aroma of petals invaded the realm of my senses.

'I believe supernatural creatures exist, but I think they've evolved the same way humans did, through generations. I don't believe in an all-knowing Creator. I think it's all genetic. Take the shapeshifter in the hotel as an example.' I cut splinters of wood away from the end of the branch as I spoke. 'He needed samples of our blood to look like us, so he must have absorbed our DNA to become our doppelgänger.'

I thought she'd be angry at me for continuing with this, but she only grinned.

'Whenever we sort this mess out, you'll go on to be a great scientist, Alice.'

A hot streak inflamed my cheeks. 'Thanks.'

'But how does your science explain vampires and what we experienced with Bella?'

When not fighting for my life, I'd given this some considerable thought.

'It's all to do with the regeneration of cells, but I don't understand how it works. I'm only sixteen, remember.'

We laughed together, and at that point, I was desperate for us to be sisters.

Cassie stared at me. 'Did you mean what you said in there about being lonely all your life? How have you endured that?'

The laughter dried up inside me. Ladybirds fluttered their red and black wings as the sun cut through the trees and caressed my face.

'It's all I've ever known, until now. And I survived by adapting to my environment.'

We sat in silence for a while, admiring our handiwork on the branches turned into stakes.

'Going back to your evolutionary theory about the supernatural, how would you explain the concept of the magical artefacts Kai mentioned? How does science ratio-nalise a Mirror of Time?'

'Quantum mechanics,' I said.

She shook her head and laughed. 'I need you on my pub quiz team. Go on, enlighten me.'

'Quantum tunnelling is an evanescent wave coupling effect that occurs in quantum mechanics. The correct wavelength combined with the proper tunnelling barrier makes it possible to pass signals, faster than light, backwards in time. Maybe that's how this mirror works.'

Cassie got up and brushed nature off her clothes. 'I suppose we might find out when we get the damn thing.' I stood and we headed the way we'd come up. 'At least it'll be easier walking down those steps.'

We strode towards a meeting with the most famous vampire in history.

We caught the sun's rays as we went and it was glorious to be outside. The stakes sat hidden inside our jackets as we walked, but considering the town's links with Dracula, I doubt they'd have elicited much response from the people we marched past.

Groups of seagulls followed us again as we moved across the river via the bridge. I observed the tourists queuing for the regular boat trips, fighting my temptation to stop for a drink and another ice cream. There was a sign for the Dracula Experience, but it pointed in the wrong direction.

I sidled up to Cassie as we strolled along.

'Are vampires afraid of the sun?' I hoped so since the closest star in the sky was blanketing us. We moved down a leafy street dotted with dozens of parked cars as I checked the house numbers, our destination a few yards ahead.

'I've never seen one in the daylight, so I guess they must be.'

'Apart from Bella, how many of them have you met?'

We stopped outside the building. 'You mean, how many have I killed? That would be two: one in Newcastle, the other in Sunderland. They were both wearing football shirts, but I doubt Dracula will do the same if he's sleeping inside there.' She nodded towards the house we'd come to break into.

'If he does, I'll bet it's a Man United top.'

Cassie pulled a face at my knowledge of football. 'It's impressive from the outside. No need to live in a dusty castle in Transylvania when you've got that.'

She was correct. The building was stunning, with a large, sumptuous walled garden filled with flowers of every vivid colour and bushes which must have been hand sculpted for the topiary. Looming trees hovered around the edge of the walls. There was no sign of life behind the windows or in the garden.

'How do we get in?'

Cassie removed a nail file from her jacket, and I wondered how many tools she had in there.

'We go to the back and open a window.'

She was over the wall before I protested. I checked the road and followed her. She'd disappeared as I stepped on to the grass. I ran after her, the stake rattling against my chest as I moved.

As I turned the corner, she had her face pressed against the glass and was sliding the nail file along the edge of the wood. The lock popped as I arrived. I grabbed her arm before she opened the window.

'Are we going to discuss a plan of action?'

Cassie curled her lips at me. 'What's there to discuss? Kill any vamps we see and find this Mirror of Time.' Everything was always straightforward with her.

'This house is massive. We can't search everywhere.'

'Why not? Dracs is sleeping, so we can do whatever we want if we dispose of his security.'

'And what if he has human guards in there? We can't

kill them.' I was reluctant to kill vampires, but there was no way I'd murder a person inside the house, or anywhere else.

'Don't worry, maybe-sister,' she said as she climbed through the window. 'I'm sure everything will be fine.'

I scrambled after her and closed the window behind me. We stepped into a living room straight from Georgian times, with its large sofas, sparkling candelabra, impressive chandelier and unlit fireplace. The only thing looking like it belonged to the twenty-first century was the sixty-inch TV next to me. The room, like the rest of the house, was clouded in silence. Had Kai given us the correct address? Had she sent us into a trap?

'Do you trust the Warwitch?'

Cassie shrugged. 'It's too late for that now. But I don't trust anyone apart from you.'

Heat spread through my face. 'Do you think he'll be in a coffin in the basement?'

The stake was in her hand. 'We'll check each room until we find him and the Mirror.'

She pressed her head to the door, listening to discover if there was anyone or anything on the other side. Cassie opened it slowly. The hinges creaked, and I reached for my weapon.

We stepped into a corridor covered by a checkerboard carpet. Stairs led up and down. I peered over the edge to see what was below and found nothing.

'Shall we split up?' I didn't want to, but it seemed like the quickest option.

'Never divide your forces when there are monsters around.'

She headed down, with me close behind, glancing up in case anyone tried to sneak up on us. The reception area was shiny and bright, with a polished wooden floor, a large leather sofa covered in cushions, a Persian rug in the middle, and many plastic plant pots. It all smelt brand new.

I stood in the centre and glanced at Cassie, wondering if she was thinking the same as I: was this a trap set by Kai? Perhaps she'd sent us here to get the Mirror of Time so she could use it herself. That trick she'd pulled with the mermaids wasn't exactly friendly.

Were we only pawns for the Warwitch?

As that thought possessed my mind, we moved into the living room. It wasn't empty.

'You're not the first people to come here in search of the impossible.'

He sat in a rocking chair, his expression a charisma-free zone, his voice designed for telling you about the late arrival of trains. Gaily coloured patterns covered the wallpaper, providing an atmosphere out of place with the extensive collection of skulls placed on bookshelves containing no books.

We stepped further into the room, stakes clutched in our fingers. Cassie spoke first.

'Are you the owner of this house?' I guessed she didn't want to name the so-called Lord of the Undead.

He spread his hands out in front of him, revealing a set of webbed tattoos on both palms.

'No, I'm only the servant to the Master.'

'You're a Familiar, a human who protects a monster.' Cassie hurled the words at him.

He turned to his side and picked up a delicate teapot. 'Would you girls like a drink?'

'Do you have the Mirror of Time?' I said.

He poured himself a drink, but it wasn't tea. I smelt the thick blood run from the porcelain and into the cup. He dropped two sugars into the scarlet liquid.

'Human blood is never sweet enough.'

He took something from the table and placed it in the cup to stir the blood: it wasn't a spoon, but a human finger. There was a wedding ring on it.

Cassie reacted quicker than me, jumping forward with the stake high above her head. She landed on an empty chair, the sharpened wood cutting through the material. I scanned the room for him, finding him crouched underneath the bordered-up window at the back. He still held the cup of blood in his hand, his little finger pointing towards the ceiling. He'd moved so fast, my brain hurt.

My maybe-sister climbed out of the seat and I stood next to her.

'We don't want to hurt you,' I said with a confidence I didn't have. He drank from the cup and placed it on the carpet. A thin ruby sliver dripped from his lips and stained the material.

'Oh, don't worry; you won't.'

He leapt at me, but Cassie got between us, shoving her shoulder into his body. They tumbled across the floor. The stake rolled from her hand and hit the bottom of the rocking chair. He was on top of her, hands around her throat, fangs growing from his mouth.

I bounded towards them, snatching Cassie's weapon from the floor. I landed on his shoulders as he was about to bite her face, plunging both stakes into his head. We fell off her on separate sides. He wailed in agony, a terrible sound like a thousand dogs screaming into the night as blood gushed from his wounds. Cassie moved like lightning, pulling out one stake as he grabbed at her. She pushed it into his ribs, forcing him back and landing on his chest.

Something inside him cracked, his neck lolling to the side as his eyes burst. A groan died in his throat. Cassie removed her largest knife and sawed at his neck. It took her three minutes to decapitate the vampire. I made sure no one else entered the room, trying not to look at what she was doing.

She threw the head into the corner and wiped the blade on his clothes.

'Well, he was quicker than I expected. The two I killed before were snails compared to him. It's a good job I've got you with me, maybe-sister.'

She removed the stake from his chest and picked up the one which had fallen from his neck. She tossed it to me. I was glad to have it back in my hand.

'So now we go through the rest of the house?'

Cassie nodded. 'I'm guessing there'll be swarms of other vamps guarding their master, so we need to be ultra-careful.'

'You've got nothing to fear from me, ladies.'

The voice made me jump as I spun around. Standing in the doorway was the most attractive man I'd ever seen.

'Welcome to my humble home. I am Dracula.'

17 THE MIRROR OF TIME

'Are you looking for this?' His voice was warm velvet. There was something in the tone of it I wanted to follow, a magnetic pull grasping for my legs. Cassie stared at him, but I shielded my face from his gaze with my arm. All I saw was the mirror he held towards us, small enough to fit into the palm of my hand, daring me to reach out and snatch it from his bony fingers. It had a silver edge around the outside, but there was nothing special about it. I'd seen fancier mirrors in Poundland.

Cassie was by my side, stake pointed at him. 'If you give it to us, we'll let you live.'

Dracula was rake thin, looking like he'd snap in half if he fell over. He looked beyond Cassie, staring at the decapitated head of his servant.

'You know, there was no need to do that. Renley would get himself overexcited at the littlest things.'

'Is that the Mirror of Time?' I said.

He ignored the question, firing back one of his own. 'Are you twin sisters?'

'Maybe,' Cassie said.

He rolled his hand over his chin. 'There's something about you two which seems very familiar, but I can't work out what it is.'

Cassie glared at him. 'We need that mirror.'

'You can't need it as much as I do, girls.'

His voice dropped into near silence. For some unknown reason, I felt sorry for him.

'Why do you want a mirror if you have no reflection?'

I assumed that piece of the folklore was correct. He held it up to his face and scrutinised the glass.

'You don't understand how annoying it is not to look at yourself.' He lowered it to his side. 'But this mirror is more important to me than that.'

'Why?' I said.

Sadness seeped from his face. 'You can never know how lonely it is being immortal and watching all those you love wither and die before your eyes.'

Cassie laughed at him. 'You can make vampires until they're running out of your nose. You can have the pick of them.'

He dismissed the idea with a wave of his emaciated hand.

'Those creatures have no souls. It's never the same. I lost my one true love years ago, and this mirror is the only way I can still see her, but even now, the connection is fading.' The sorrow drained from him like water from a leaky tap.

Kai's words about using the Mirror to peer into time came back to me.

'You look into it to see the people you've lost.'

Raised fingers covered my eyes in case he tried some supernatural mind control. How quickly my rational brain had been turned to mush by this man.

He addressed me. 'You can look at me, child. I won't hypnotise you.'

I didn't believe in this nonsense. My will was stronger than his. I dropped my hand and stared at him.

'I'm not afraid of you.'

'That's better.' That voice was audible chocolate. 'Now, tell me: am I handsome?'

His fingers were delicate and pale, brushing across his cheeks and under his cerulean eyes.

'You're the most beautiful man I've ever seen.'

I couldn't help myself, the words slipping from my mouth. His expression was intense, blue eyes sparkling like a supernova, his bone structure stolen from Adonis. His lips glistened with a pout Mick Jagger would have died for.

'Thank you, child.'

He gazed around the room, lingering on the head of the vampire we'd killed. He didn't seem upset by that. Then he stared at us.

'How the world must have changed in fifty years if two teenage girls could murder my most faithful follower.' He seemed impressed with our actions. 'Why do you want the Mirror of Time?'

Cassie brandished her knife in his direction. 'That's our business, not yours. Give it to me and I'll kill you quickly.'

His laugh was like a kitten purring. 'No, not now you won't. Today, you were my alarm clock.'

I put my hand on Cassie's arm to lower the blade. 'What do you mean?'

He wore a purple and gold waistcoat and reached into his right pocket to retrieve a small envelope. He offered it to me. I was reluctant to take it, my mind conjuring up all sorts of nonsense like I'd be bound to him forever if I did. Then I remembered I'm a scientist and snatched it from his hands.

His nails were perfectly manicured, and I resisted the urge to ask him who'd been doing them for the last five decades. I stifled my shaking fingers and opened the envelope.

Cassie raised the knife again. 'What does it say?'

'Today's date is written on it.'

'You two are my alarm clock. A being of tremendous knowledge presented that to me fifty years ago and said I'd be woken on the date by intruders in my home.'

'Who gave you this?' I couldn't tell if he was playing with us or not.

'That, I'm not at liberty to reveal. But I'll hand you the Mirror of Time if you both promise me one thing.'

I stared at Cassie, but she didn't take her eyes from him.

'What do you want?' I said.

'If both of you swear you'll never harm me, I'll give you what you desire.'

Cassie laughed. 'You think we'll kill you now?'

He grinned in return as his hand went into the other pocket of his waistcoat and removed another envelope.

'Well, you've already threatened me at least once, and it's possible my long sleep will arrive today, but I don't believe so. Inside this is the date of my death. I'm to be killed by whoever woke me up.'

'Us?' I couldn't hide my surprise.

'It would appear so. But if you both promise never to harm me, then the prophecy will never come to pass.'

I considered his words, was forming the only reply I could think of when Cassie spoke first.

'No. I make no promises with monsters.'

I didn't believe in prophecies. 'We must, Cassie, if we want the Mirror.'

'No. We kill him now and take it from him. He already said we're fated to end him.'

She had a point. But I didn't like the way he was grinning at me.

'Follow me upstairs.' He was out of the room before we could reply.

I turned to Cassie.

'What shall we do?'

She moved to the door. 'Dracula has the Mirror, so we have to get it off him.' She stepped outside, with me a few seconds after her. He stood at the top of the stairs, smiling at us.

'Meet me where you broke in,' he shouted down, only it wasn't a shout, more like a rasping echo played through an over-tuned violin. We had no choice, moving up the stairs and into the room where Cassie had broken into the house. Whispering shadows moved somewhere in the corner of my eye, and I gripped tightly to the stake. A cold breeze drifted in from the open window, bringing with it a fragrance of orange petals.

'Tell me why we shouldn't kill you right now and take the Mirror from your corpse?'

Cassie's assertiveness was impressive. She appeared confident most of the time, but I hadn't seen this measure of strength from her before.

Dracula dabbed his chin. 'Look at the window ledge.'

I hesitated, thinking it was a trap, but Cassie kept her eyes on him as I did so. A raven sat at the open window with a piece of paper tied at its throat.

'How long do you think it will take for the bird to fly to Greece?'

'What?' I looked at him.

'If you've come for the Mirror of Time, then you'll need the Eye of Medusa next. If I die, the bird will rush to the Gorgon with a warning around its neck.'

'I don't trust you.' Cassie thrust her dagger towards him. 'You want us dead. You could already have warned her.'

'I promise you, children, I have not, and the Lord of the Undead's word is his bond.'

He was exerting his authority, reminding us of his position, and ours. He might be the most famous vampire in history, but he was still an adult out to intimidate me, and I'd spent all my life dealing with people like that.

I whispered into Cassie's ear. 'We have to do it.'

She shook her head. 'Let him send the raven. With the blade Kai has, we can cut through space and be on the island well before the bird gets there.'

'We can't risk it. Plus, we'd have to fight to get the Mirror, and even with the two of us and him not looking too good, there's no guarantee we'd beat him.'

A smirk crossed my maybe-sister's face. 'I'll take the risk.'

I stepped away from her, my focus returning to him, not wanting to settle on his gaze for too long.

'We'll do it. I promise never to harm you.'

'No,' Cassie shouted. 'I won't do such a thing.'

I turned to her. 'We have no choice, not if we want that Mirror. And we do.'

I watched steam come from her ears. Dracula took a nail file from his pocket and showered attention on those perfect cuticles. He pretended to stare at the ceiling, but I knew he observed the silent communication between Cassie and me. I gripped her fingers and peered deep into her eyes.

'I promise,' Cassie said.

'Thank you.' Dracula gave an exaggerated bow. I put my hand on Cassie's arm before she tried to decapitate him. He removed a parchment from his pocket and took a pen from the table in the room. 'This paper states you've promised never to harm the bearer of this contract. I need the two of you to sign it. Then I'll give you the Mirror of Time.'

He handed the paper and pen to me. I read it out.

'We, the undersigned, solemnly swear never to harm the bearer of this document on pain of death for us and all our relatives.'

I didn't hesitate, placing the contract on the table and signing it. I gave the pen to Cassie and waited. She took it and did nothing but glare at him, the Lord of the Vampires. Outside of that melodic voice, there wasn't anything impressive about him. Well, apart from those handsomely sculpted cheekbones and magnetic eyes. I put my hand in hers and squeezed her fingers. I kept staring at his face, hearing his voice, even though I fought against it.

'We have no choice,' I whispered to her.

She pressed the pen into the paper and signed. I took the contract and held it close to my chest. Something flashed beneath Dracula's gaze and I couldn't work out what it was. His lips shivered as he spoke.

'Do you desire to look into your past?' He waited for a reply we didn't give. 'Or do you want more than that?' He placed the Mirror against his cheek, and my rational brain vanished down a rabbit hole as I imagined him somehow falling through the glass and disappearing. In an instant, his expression changed from joy to trepidation, the sparkle in his eyes replaced with devouring darkness. 'You want to travel back in time to discover the secrets of your birth.'

I moved the contract away from my body. 'Is it possible to do that?'

He placed the Mirror at his side. 'Not only is it possible, but it's also dangerous. If you go back in time, you'll awaken forces too terrible to contemplate. I would advise against it.

Use the Mirror to view, nothing else.' There was a near-imperceptible shake in his finger, which he tried to conceal, but I saw it.

'Why have you slept for fifty years?' Cassie said. I was thankful for her changing the subject. He tapped the Mirror against his leg. Dark shadows grew across his face and obscured his eyes.

'A century of loneliness consumed my soul, so I needed rest and refuge. You cannot contemplate what isolation does to an immortal when all that surrounds you is empty and vacuous.'

My heart ached at his words, legs wanting to stumble forward to throw my arms around his withered frame. My brain stopped me from doing something so foolish.

'What will you do now you're awake?' Was he our responsibility because we'd reintroduced him to the world?

The smile returned to his face. 'I have half a century of new things to explore, all thanks to you two.' They were innocent words, but they made me shudder. Dracula handed me the Mirror of Time. 'I believe this is yours.'

When I took it from his hand, he ran a finger over my skin. Ice drifted down my spine and stabbed at the whole of my body as I gave him the contract. Cassie scowled next to me before glaring at him.

'I could still kill you.'

He looked disappointed. 'You'd break your word even though you got what you came for?' He gazed right at her. 'How did you misplace a part of an ear? Did one of my children do that to you?'

Cassie's hand shook, the blade trembling in her fingers. I touched her arm and stared at him.

'We'll keep our word. Now move so we can leave.'

The raven had disappeared from the open window. I

could have rushed him and forced him backwards, out of the gap and into the sun. It was a fleeting thought, quickly crushed because I knew I wouldn't break my promise.

I smiled at Cassie. When I turned my gaze back to him, he was gone. There was no way out of the room apart from the window, and the door was behind us.

'Parlour tricks,' Cassie said as she climbed through the gap to the outside. As I followed her, I understood what people meant when they said someone was walking over your grave.

We left the grounds of the house quicker than when we'd come. It was early afternoon and the sun had dropped lower in the sky to bake everything silly enough to fall under its yellow eyes. Being outside in the daytime didn't make me feel any safer from an unexpected attack from the man, the vampire, we'd bargained with.

I clasped the Mirror of Time, but didn't look into the glass, worried what might happen if I did. Cassie stood in the middle of the garden, staring at the house. I wondered if she thought it would collapse in on itself. I brushed my hand against hers.

'Do we take this back to Kai?'

Her eyelids fell with a slight lolling of her head as if she was about to drop off.

'Do you trust the Warwitch?'

I pulled her away from the building, concerned it was hypnotising her into drowsiness.

'We have no choice. Kai was right about Dracula and the Mirror. We must make sure we use all of their expertise. You might have been doing this for two years, but it's all new to me.' And my brain was having a continuous battle with what was real and what wasn't.

We moved through the garden and clambered over the

wall at the front of the house, finding the street deserted. We headed back to the church and the Impossible Palace the same way we'd come. I didn't look forward to climbing those steps again, so we stopped halfway there to have a drink outside a café. Old people baked in the heat, tempting me to push an ice cube across my forehead. I sipped at the fruit juice, letting the cold of the glass cool my beating heart. The Mirror of Time was safely concealed inside my jacket, which I refused to take off even though my brain screamed at me to do so.

Cassie raised her drink to me. 'That's one down with three to go.'

It was a promising start, having fronted up to Dracula, survived and got what we needed.

Now, all we had to do was steal a snake from a Gorgon's head.

18 THE EYE OF MEDUSA

When we reached the top of the steps, as my heart thumped against my ribs, Kai was waiting there for us. She was sprawled out underneath the trees where we'd crafted our makeshift stakes. I pressed my hand against my chest to calm my nerves, feeling the edge of the Mirror inside my jacket.

'Did you sense our energy coming up here?'

There were no birds following us this time. She sat up with a jolt. Rufus crept from behind a tree, a mouse struggling between his lips.

'There was no need for that. I heard you wheezing and coughing all the way.'

'We got what you sent us for, so what's next?' Cassie sounded in no mood for frivolity.

Rufus hurried over to me, dropped the now dead mouse at my feet, and then strolled back to Kai, who bundled him up in those delicate arms.

'Did you kill Dracula?'

'No,' I said, sensing Cassie's angry eyes burrowing into my head. 'We struck a deal to get the Mirror of Time.'

Kai scratched under the cat's hairy chin. Rufus continued to stare at me as if I was the fly and he was a spider.

'Well, that's unusual. It's never wise to bargain with the Lord of the Undead, but at least he's left this town, which is a weight off my mind. Come, I'll show you some of the abbey.'

She turned from where we'd entered the Impossible Palace the last time and headed through the cemetery.

We jogged to catch up, my legs cursing me from the recent exertions to get so high above the town.

'Do you know where every supernatural creature is in Whitby?' I said as we strode either side of the Warwitch. She grinned as she spoke.

'I have a map on the wall with pins in it for non-human things. And Dracula disappeared from it about an hour ago.'

'Really?' I had one eye on her and the other on my feet, trying to avoid holes in the ground, broken stones and any big clumps of grass which could trip me up in an instant.

'No,' she laughed. 'It's all up here.' She tapped her head.

'How does that work?' Cassie said. The birds returned as a murder of crows this time, not seagulls, hovering at a respectable distance. 'Is it like what you did to us with the mermaids?'

Kai walked and talked. 'Certain Celestials, ones of significant power and influence, emit energy which people like me are susceptible to. Think of it as a GPS signal on your phone.'

We strode in between tombstones, approaching the ruins of the abbey. I glanced at Cassie.

'What about us; do you get anything from Cassie and me?'

'As I told you earlier, you two are a blank spot on my

radar.'

The sea and the horizon were on our left as we exited the cemetery, making our way through the tourists and striding towards the former monastery.

'Are we not heading back to the Impossible Palace?' My legs yearned for a rest.

Kai pointed into the sky, where the crows grouped as if blocked from going any further.

'Once we get beyond there and into the heart of the abbey, I'll answer all your questions.'

I rubbed at the itch on my wrist. 'All of them?'

She grinned at me. 'Well, maybe most of them.'

Cassie's face resembled the grumpiest of cats. 'I need a proper meal before we go gallivanting off to Greece.'

'Actually, Medusa's island prison is closer to Libya.' Kai stared into the distance at a queue outside the abbey.

I struggled to find any money in my pockets. 'Do we have to pay to enter?'

Kai touched her nose. 'You two get in free with me.'

Cassie's stomach rumbled. 'As long as I eat soon.'

We were outside the perimeter wall, watching the queue increase. The Warwitch strode to the front, accosted neither by the staff nor the public. We followed her and slipped inside the grounds.

'These are not the girls you're looking for,' Cassie said as she beamed at me. I was happy to see her happy.

As we entered, people were watching a play. It looked like a scene from Stoker's book as a heavily made-up Dracula, including long cloak and even longer fangs, terrorised a group of kids. A surge of wind swept across the abbey, pushing bodies forward and into each other. The guy playing Dracula looked nothing like the real thing.

The architecture and sheer size of the ruins amazed me.

'This must have been an impressive site before it was broken.'

Kai walked towards the far side, away from the noise of the visitors, and stood under a large archway. 'Invading Danes and Vikings damaged the original monastery on these grounds. In the 13th century, it was rebuilt in a Gothic style, which took about two hundred years. Henry VIII destroyed this second monastery in 1540 during the Dissolution of the Monasteries. The ravages of the weather and time have left it in this state.' She held out her hands, Rufus lurking behind her. 'Come with me, and you'll see it in all of its former glory.'

I took her hand without hesitation, Cassie more reluctantly. Everything disappeared around us: the sky, the grounds, all the people, and the ruins. We were inside a covered hall, with the ancient stone restored and glorious stained-glass windows reflecting in the light. A large table stood in the middle of the room, laden with food bowls, and from the smell, it was the same Bolognese I'd had earlier. Cassie didn't wait, darting forward to grab a bowl of sauce and a plate of pasta. I joined her, picking at the bread and cheese. I removed the Mirror of Time and placed it on the table.

Kai stared at Cassie. 'When did you recognise the supernatural was all around you?'

Cassie wiped food from her face, gulping water from a glass as she considered the question.

'I think I've always known, but I hid it from myself as much as everyone else. Only when people started dying did I do something about it.' She scratched at the missing part of her ear.

The Warwitch turned to me. 'I suspect you continue with doubts, Alice.'

I nibbled at the cheese. 'I believe the supernatural is real now because I've seen ample evidence for it.'

'But you think there are scientific explanations for everything you've witnessed.'

'I'm still searching for answers.' The bread was dry as it trundled down my throat.

'How would your science explain this?' Kai brandished the Blade of Reality in the air. Her hand dashed through the ether as if her fingers were gyrating in a dancehall. The knife cut right, then down before moving left and up again. When she finished, Kai peeled back reality, and we peered through to a place on the other side of the world. Tomato sauce dripped from Cassie's mouth and on to the table, her eyes bulging from her head. Rufus jumped up and licked at the mess Cassie had made.

A thick wad of cheese broke between my teeth. I chewed on it for two minutes before speaking, watching the gap shimmer like electricity jumping in the air. Where she'd cut into space should have looked upon a brick wall and the bottom of an ornate window, but now, all I saw was the middle parts and legs of a group of statues.

'I have no answer to that,' I said as I swallowed the potent cheddar.

'I'll close this after you go through. Then you have thirty minutes to get the Eye before I open it again.'

'Why can't you leave it open?' Cassie appeared annoyed at the idea of us trapped on the other side. The section Kai had cut into flapped over its edge, a breeze coming from the gap she'd made. It wasn't large enough to walk through without arching your back. The temperature increased around that point, the hairs on my arm feeling the warm air.

'If the Gorgon gets over here, she'll cause untold damage before she's stopped. I'm not leaving that window open while you're on the island. You've got thirty minutes; any longer, and there's no way back for you two. You'll be another set of statues staring out to sea.'

I grabbed the Mirror and moved from the table, a slice of crusty bread between my fingers, to get a closer view inside the gap. I slipped the Mirror into my jacket. I bent a little, twisting to peer at a man clutching a shield in one hand, a sword in the other; his features were contorted in agony, mouth wide open, eyes frozen into nothingness. I couldn't see the face of the other statue because a large helmet covered his head.

'They're not statues, are they?'

'That's your fate if you're not careful.'

I moved from the gap, possessed by a sudden fear something would come sprinting through for me.

'I thought Perseus killed Medusa?'

Kai scooped Rufus from the table. 'That was a myth created by man to bolster his image. Humans separated Medusa from her sisters by trickery, and then exiled her to Sarpedon. The island is hidden by magic, but the occasional ship finds its way there, and a few hunters have discovered her prison. None of them has ever left there alive.'

'We'll make it back.' I lowered my head and stepped through the space Kai had made with the knife. Cassie followed me.

'I'll cut here again in thirty minutes. If you're not waiting on the other side, I'll close it immediately.' Her voice drifted away as she returned reality to its proper point, the gap popping back into place like a chewing gum bubble in reverse.

'Do we have a plan?' Cassie said.

We were pressed against the wall, hands ready to shield our heads if the Gorgon appeared. Concrete men surrounded us, faces twisted in shock and agony, or arms thrust forward to protect their eyes. Did they know what they were getting into, or did they stumble into their frozen deaths? I scanned everyone and found no women among them. Were we the first to come here since people separated Medusa from her sisters?

'In the myth, she's beheaded by Perseus as he uses a mirrored shield to see where she is.'

'We don't need a shield or some bloke to help us.'

Cassie stormed away from me and down the corridor. There was no thought of safety or danger. Two years of killing things had made her reckless. Lizards and snakes crept and slithered across the floor. The aroma of the sea drifted around the corner.

'Wait,' I whispered. 'If you bump into her, she'll turn you to stone.'

I grabbed her by the shoulder as I caught up with her. She scowled as we reached the entrance of a large chamber. Even though it was a sweltering summer's day, torches burnt along the wall, and roaring braziers stood across the floor. Rubble was scattered everywhere. Some of it was rock dislodged from the ceiling or columns holding up the building; other parts were bits of bodies turned hard and grey: arms, legs, eyeless heads, and everything in-between. I twisted from them and gazed at Cassie, who was looking around the room, scanning every nook and cranny.

'Has it crossed your mind, Alice, that Kai is lying to us and she won't send us back in time?'

'You think she's sent us after these artefacts so she can use them for herself?'

Cassie stared straight ahead as she nodded. 'Sure, because that's what I'd do: get someone to do your dirty work for you, especially when it's that dangerous.'

Before I could reply, the sound of hissing snakes echoed off the concrete. Then, a large shadow slithered across the floor in the distance. I dragged Cassie into me and dropped my voice as low as possible.

'We need to think this through.'

She pushed me away. 'I already have.'

Cassie pulled a black scarf from her pocket and tied it around her face.

'What, you'll confront her blindfolded?'

'I've been trained for this.'

The hissing was closer, a shadow drifting towards us as we hugged the wall. I pressed my lips to Cassie's ear.

'You've been trained to fight in the dark? Who by?'

'It doesn't matter.'

She pushed off me and turned to face the creature. The Gorgon's cry was a high piercing shriek that burned my ears. I fell to the floor, hands over my head. A whooshing sensation filled my senses as my brain rattled against my skull. The noise travelled to my eyes and blurred my vision, and it was as if I was underwater in the dark.

I wanted to scream, but dragged myself up instead, banging my shoulder into the wall in an attempt to rid that horrible sound from my head. My fingers shook as I reached into my jacket and removed the Mirror of Time. My eyesight flickered back to normal as I held the Mirror out to the side, peering at the reflection as my ears stopped burning. Cassie and Medusa faced each other. Rubble was between them, and I did not understand how my maybe-sister could avoid those obstacles and defeat the thing glaring at her.

Tiny snakes dropped from Medusa's writhing head, slithering across the stone and towards Cassie, who never moved. I grabbed a torch from the wall and hurled it into the mass of creatures converging on her. They screamed as they burned, and so did their mother.

The Mirror shook in my hand as the Gorgon slid forward, the lower half of her body one long serpentine shape, slithering over the stones towards Cassie. I watched in horror as the snakes on Medusa's head snapped and bit at Cassie. She must have heard the attacks, moving backwards and sideways to avoid the threat, dodging the obstacles on the ground with practised ease. The Gorgon moved slower than I expected, Cassie more skilled in the dark than I would have thought possible. Fear raced through me, my mind struggling to find a way to help her.

I screamed as Medusa lunged and caught Cassie on the arm with her long nails raking down Cassie's skin. The Gorgon turned towards me and I saw her face in full in the Mirror. Wings flapped from her back; a violent scarlet consumed her eyes; twitching living venomous snakes in place of hair; a vicious shriek vibrating from her blood-red lips. As her image burnt into my mind, Medusa froze to the spot. It was enough for Cassie to grab her by the neck and push the creature to the floor. Medusa was larger than her, but Cassie appeared to possess superhuman strength, forcing the Gorgon down and to the ground. The snakes on her head writhed in a frenzy, her arms clawing and grasping to no avail as Cassie readied for the kill.

'No!' My arm was across my face as I ran to them. 'Don't do it, Cassie.' The Mirror was in my other hand, reflecting Medusa's startled gaze as I moved behind her.

'What?' Cassie shouted. She had the knife pressed against Medusa's skin, ready to cut the head from the body.

I didn't address my maybe-sister, but the creature. 'Medusa, will you turn your eyes away from us and promise to stay like that if we spare your life?'

'Are you mad, Alice?'

I ignored Cassie's question, staring into the Mirror as the Gorgon's face transformed from horror into confusion. The snakes stopped squirming, settling on Medusa's head as if they were strands of hair. Cassie's knife cut into flesh and a trickle of blood swam down that scaled neck. The Gorgon didn't react.

'Will you do it, Medusa?' I wasn't even sure if she understood what I said. Her ruby eyes flickered for a second before she nodded and turned her gaze to the floor. Cassie must have felt the movement against her knife.

'What are you doing, Alice?'

'Remove the blade, Cassie; please trust me.'

My heart was throbbing so hard, I expected it to burst through my chest. We could die if I got this wrong. The only thing breaking the silence was the gentle hum of the snakes. I stared at the back of the Gorgon's head, ready in case she turned around. Cassie's breathing was heavy, her eyes hidden behind that scarf, so I couldn't work out what she was thinking.

'All right,' Cassie said.

I watched her pull the knife away and remove the blindfold. In that instant, I could have doomed my maybe-sister to a terrible death, but she trusted me. My heart continued to hammer at a thousand beats per second. Medusa's head faced the stone, the snakes sniffing at the dirt and dust. Cassie stared at her, and then at me.

'Go to the exit point, Cassie. I'll meet you there.'

She didn't argue or hesitate. I lifted my arm across my face and pointed the Mirror at an angle towards the ground.

Then I moved forward and presented my offer to the Gorgon.

TRANSPORTING the generator took longer than I expected, but using the Blade of Reality made it easier than it would have been.

'What exactly have you bought with my credit card?' Cassie bristled with annoyance, but I guessed she was impressed with my bartering skills. She sipped a cold beer that Kai had produced from nowhere.

I gave her a list of what I'd bought. 'Three giant TV screens, a surround sound system, continuous rolling payment for the internet and twelve months subscription to Netflix, Amazon and Disney; plus the generator which we must replace in a year.'

'And you bought all this because of what you saw in that monster's eyes?'

I contained my annoyance. 'She's no monster. If only a fraction of the Gorgon myth is true, then Medusa was wronged before her solitary imprisonment on that island. What I witnessed in her face was loneliness, isolation and frustration. I know exactly how she feels, but I haven't had centuries for those emotions to fester.' And perhaps I'd found a sister while she'd lost two, though I didn't tell Cassie that. 'All she needed was someone to connect with, to understand her, not people viewing her like a beast and trying to kill her.'

'You made friends with a monster; how novel.'

I refused to argue with Cassie, staring at Kai instead. She sat in an oversized chair and stroked Rufus's head. She appeared pleased we'd returned from the island in one piece; and that we hadn't needed to slay the Gorgon. But I still wasn't sure if I trusted her.

'Oh, she also has a mobile phone with a rolling contract

paid for on direct debit.'

'She has a phone?' Cassie nearly spat her drink all over me. 'Who is she going to call?'

'Me. I bought a new mobile for myself and gave her my number. I'm not sure how she understands English, but she does.' Kai watched me in astonishment; even the cat smiled at me. 'And I set her up on a few internet forums.'

Cassie shook her head and slumped into the comfiest seat she could find. 'I can't wait to hear about this.'

I pulled up a chair as all three of us sat around the table in the grand hall. Rufus jumped from Kai's hands and sneaked across the wood.

'Using the Mirror, I showed Medusa how to use the internet. A few sites are dedicated to followers of Greek myths, including a couple for worshipers of the Gorgons. I got her signed up for those. When I left her, she was sending out memes of Zeus falling off a mountain.'

Kai clapped her hands. 'How marvellous, but I doubt you'll have this much fun in Hollywood.'

I took out my new phone and sent Medusa a text. 'We need sleep first. This has been a hectic day, what with Dracula in the morning, Medusa in the afternoon, and then all that shopping.'

Cassie finished her drink with a loud burp. 'I bet you enjoyed shopping the most.'

Kai grabbed the empty bottle and dropped it into an invisible bin.

'Do you want separate rooms?'

'Yes,' we said in stereo.

I got up and followed Kai from the room. The Mirror of Time was in one pocket, while in another was a warm bag containing what I'd bargained from Medusa: a sleeping snake cut from her head.

19   LOST IN HOLLYWOOD

Thankfully, our sleeping quarters were not the living arrangements of a fifteenth-century monastery: Kai led me into what she described as re-imagined Victoriana. Extravagant hand-painted murals covered the walls and the ceiling; elaborate nature-inspired designs of flowering trees, brightly coloured bushes, and a swathe of sea and sand rose from behind the king-sized four-poster bed. If I hadn't known any better, I'd have sworn I was outside. I was asleep as soon as my head hit the pillow.

When I woke, it was as if I'd been plugged into the electricity for the night and was recharged and raring to go. Kai delivering breakfast in bed was another pleasant surprise. After I'd eaten, showered and dressed, I went downstairs to meet the others; and this time, the stairs didn't defy gravity and go in every direction. I couldn't take that again, especially with those horrible human-headed giant insects crawling around.

Cassie sat drinking coffee, the aroma of it surging up my nose and kick-starting my synapses. I preferred tea, but the strong caffeine smell always got my bones bouncing.

'Are you ready to meet some genuine movie stars, maybe-sister?'

I was refreshed, clean, and fed. What else was there to do?

'Where are we going?'

Kai sat opposite Cassie, the Blade of Reality resting on the table. I'd left the Mirror of Time and the Eye of Medusa in my room.

'Our actors are filming a TV version of Sodom and Gomorrah in Los Angeles.'

'That seems appropriate.' Cassie laughed.

'The producers wanted to digitise everything apart from the actors, but our friends insisted on having sets built for every scene.'

I'd never been interested in movies and television, much preferring my fiction on the page.

'Perhaps they're striving for authenticity?'

'Hardly; it gives them a filming location, and that attracts adoring fans. They feed off that. I can get you there whenever you're ready.'

'You make it sound so easy, Kai. Will it be?'

'It seems unlikely. You won't be able to use your charm on these two. Both angels and demons are ten times stronger than humans. How can you overcome that?' It was a question I'd pondered since I'd sealed the deal with Medusa. 'Especially considering angels keep their wings hidden unless they want you to see them.'

'Horse tranquillisers,' Cassie said.

'What?' I poured a cup of green tea and dropped a slice of lemon into it. Kai had thought of everything for our stay.

'They may be super strong, but if we shoot them with enough tranquilliser, it should knock them out.'

I had my doubts. 'And where will we get these tranquillisers from?'

'We steal them using Kai's magic knife.'

Kai picked up the Blade of Reality. 'I'll be right back.'

We watched her cut a doorway out of empty air and step through it. She closed it behind her and we waited. I removed my phone and checked the messages from Medusa. She'd sent me over a dozen during the night, and I wondered if she ever slept.

I read through them as Cassie petted Rufus; it appeared the two of them had become friends while I slumbered. Most of Medusa's texts were about what she'd found on the internet, creating a Twitter account and considering starting a blog. She craved to tell the world the truth about her life, of how she was abused and abandoned and wanted my opinion.

I replied to that message.

You should do that. Tell the world your story. I want to hear it. I bet loads of others will as well.

I also sent her links to self-help groups about depression and surviving abuse. The date on the phone made me think: it was only three days since I'd met Cassie in the park. I checked the internet to see if there was progress with the events at my flat, but the investigation couldn't identify what had killed my neighbours and the others. I still needed to know who was behind it to figure out what had slaughtered Bob and Terry.

Cassie picked up Rufus and sat next to me. The cat hissed as his fur touched my skin.

'I've been researching these actors online, Joy Canto and her husband, Patrick Snow. According to Kai, she's the demon, and he's the angel. To get into character for the movie, they're living inside a reconstruction of the Temple of Sodom.'

As I wondered what that would look like, Kai returned, the knife cutting into our location only a few feet away from me. She handed me a plastic bag as she sealed up the gap. I emptied the contents on to the table: two larger than normal handguns and half a dozen darts.

'That should be enough,' Kai said as I picked up a dart. 'Inside, there's a combination of Fentanyl and Midazolam. Injected into the vein, it should have a knock-out effect between two and five minutes after entering the bloodstream.'

Cassie grabbed one gun. 'Two minutes to sedate a demon leaves us in a lot of trouble, never mind having to deal with an angel.'

Kai readied the Blade of Reality, but I didn't know if we were ready.

'You girls are so resourceful. I'm sure you'll think of something.'

She held the Blade out and waited for our response. I slipped a dart into the gun, put more into my pocket, and then checked the time on my phone.

'It's nine o'clock now, so it's one in the morning in Los Angeles.'

'They'll be tucked up in bed and snoozing like babies, so perfect timing for you.'

I knew little about the lifestyles of film stars, but I doubted they'd be sleeping. With no nod from us, Kai sliced through the air and cut a doorway into the movie set. When we returned, if we returned, I had to ask her how the Blade knew precisely where to slice into other parts of the world.

'How long do we get?' I whispered to her.

'Thirty minutes,' she said as she sealed the gap behind us.

We strode into a different realm, one created from imagination and shaky historical records. Everything appeared golden, but a faint yellow paint fell away when I ran my fingers over the walls. To our right was a partition covered in fake hieroglyphics, while up ahead were stairs leading towards another level, guarded by two giant stone lions. They gazed at us as we made our way up.

Noises came from upstairs. Cassie and I clutched our guns. I'd met Dracula and befriended Medusa, yet it seemed strange I was about to shoot an angel and demon full of sedatives. And what would we do while we waited for the mixture to take effect?

'What if we can't see the angel's wings?' I whispered as we crept up the stairs.

'Even if they're invisible, they must be on his back. I'll hack away until I get something.' Cassie had her gun pointed in front of her. I did the same.

I admired her confidence. I stared at my maybe-sister as we went. I'd only been doing this for a short time and was a bag of nerves every single day I got out of bed, knowing what was out there. She'd been doing this for years, and on her own. What had it done to her? As we moved closer, the voices grew louder.

'You need to eat, love. It's been days.' It was a male voice, powerful and assertive. I assumed it was the angel.

'You know the camera puts pounds on me, and I have to keep my figure.' That was a female voice, demure and dismissive. I found it ironic even celestial beings could so easily fall into predictable human gender roles. Perhaps Hollywood does that to everyone.

Cassie got to the top of the steps and paused. When I

joined her, I saw why. This next level was as modern as you could get. There were no ancient trappings there, only giant screens and rows of booze. Our targets sat on a sofa. Between them was a young man, not much older than us. His eyes were glazed as he leant into the leather of the seat.

'I insist you feed now, my love. We have stunts to film later, and you'll need all your strength.' He took her hand and an expression of utter devotion flew between them.

She nodded as he removed two items from his pocket. They looked like clear plastic straws. The boy between them continued to gaze into space. The angel handed his demon love one straw and they placed them on the boy's wrists. Then they plunged them down.

I gasped. They didn't move, staring at each other. I waited for the blood to stream into the plastic, but there was nothing. Then they leant forward together and wrapped their lips around the tip of each straw. My stomach shivered. I wanted to throw up. Still, nothing came through the straw; at least, nothing I could see. But something must have done. The boy's face collapsed. His skin shrivelled, cheekbones distorted, blood seeping from his eyes. He turned into a bag of bones in front of us. Horror transfixed me.

But Cassie wasn't. She leapt from the top of the stairs, firing the gun. As the darts punctured the woman's neck, I was a few seconds behind, aiming for the man.

But those seconds were too many.

And that was no man.

He was an angel, and I saw him in all of his glory. Light burst from his every pore, wings spread out in defiance. He blinded me before I hit the ground. He kicked the gun from my hand and punched me in the ribs. Bones cracked and an explosion of pain ripped through me. Blood rushed up to my throat and invaded my mouth. I was drowning in myself when I was thrust in the air and on to the floor again. My right leg snapped. A vast weight stamped on my foot and crushed it. When the darkness came, it was the sweetest relief of my life.

THERE WAS nothing broken when I woke, only a faint memory of something terrible. I was more surprised by the fact I was alive.

'You can thank me later.' Angel eyes peered at me as angel fingers dabbed at my cheek. His wings had vanished. 'I healed all your wounds. We couldn't have you dying on me when my sweet needs your soul to get her out of this trance you evil girls have trapped her in.'

I looked beyond him. The dead boy was gone. The cocktail of drugs Cassie had emptied into her had stupefied the demon woman. Cassie sat tied and gagged to a chair, her eyes closed.

'If you've hurt her,' I said with defiance I didn't have. He ignored my words.

'She gets so fixated by perceptions of beauty and expectations of what a woman should look like. I keep telling her she should be above such petty human considerations, but I can't convince her. We've been in this Hollywood bubble for too long.' His voice was dreamlike, drifting in and out of my focus like old radio stations.

I scanned the room for a means of escape. I wasn't tied up, but was in pain, the veins in my arms and legs throbbing against my bones. I guessed it was that which made him overconfident, because why would he fear a sixteen-year-old girl? I had to keep him talking before he stuck those straws into Cassie and me.

My eyes peered into his. 'You've been famous actors for five years. Surely a demon and an angel could survive that long?'

He arched his eyebrows at me in surprise. He was handsome like most movie stars, but he didn't have that magnetic something I'd experienced with Dracula. His voice was harsh this time.

'I thought the two of you were another couple of crazed fans, but you know of the reality of life, don't you?'

'More than you'll ever realise.' I hoped I sounded more confident than I felt.

He laughed in my face. 'No, child. You know less than you think if you believe what you see are the true forms of angels and demons. You saw a little of mine earlier, but the truth of it would send you mad. My sweet and I have been an acting couple since the dawn of cinema. We were drawn to those first flickering images like moths to a flame and fell into eternal love in front of those nascent movie cameras. Can you guess which famous Hollywood couples we've been?'

He was enjoying himself, and I hated it. I flexed my fingers without him noticing.

'I have no interest in movies or Hollywood history. Was one of you a big ape?'

He cackled like a hyena, teeth so brilliant white we could only be in America.

'Child, it matters not considering how little time you have left.' He grabbed hold of my arm. 'At least take some comfort that you and your twin will keep us in Hollywood beyond these current meat suits we inhabit.'

I tried to wriggle free of his grasp, but couldn't. He pushed me against the sofa and then picked up the straws.

'Cassie,' I shouted, but she was out cold.

'Come, my love; you need to drink now.'

He dragged his demon wife to Cassie, and I could do nothing but watch him thrust the plastic into the vein in her wrist. Cassie's eyes bulged and she strained against the gag with her teeth. Then he turned to me. I threw a punch at his face, but had less strength than I thought. He held me down and grinned.

'I couldn't have you dying on me, not when I need what you have. The reconstruction job I did on your body will take about an hour to heal. It's a shame, for you, that is because I made some improvements. You'll be like the Bionic Woman, but without the metal. It's all organic and good for the environment.'

Lead weights had replaced my arms. 'What are you going to do? You're not a vampire, and I'm sure angels don't drink blood.' I was clueless about the appetites of angels.

He appeared offended by my words. 'Gracious, no. How horrible it must be to live as one of those creatures. I don't understand what God was doing half the time with some of the things the Creator spewed into this world.' He leant over me, a hand on my chest to keep me pacified. 'All Celestials feed on human souls, in some way or another. We don't need them to live, but they taste so darn good.' He laughed again. 'It's an ironic by-product of God's flawed design work. Like you humans eating chicken, I suppose.'

'I'm a vegetarian,' I said as I struggled against his weight.

He pushed the straw into my wrist and I screamed. I hadn't screamed since I was six. I was embarrassed by my weakness, ashamed I'd let Cassie down. If I'd been quicker with the darts, none of this would have happened.

I watched as the demon lowered her head over Cassie's hand.

'I could lie to you and say this will be painless and over quickly, but I won't, and it won't.'

I smelt the drool on his lips as he sucked at my flesh. A disturbing surge of electric shock infected every atom of me. My veins were ready to burst into flames, my organs and bones on the verge of splitting apart. My eyes glazed over and I waited for death.

But it never came.

———

'ALICE, Alice. Get off the floor and get me out of these restraints.' My fingers shivered as I wiped them across my face. When the light came to me, Cassie shouted again. 'Alice, get a move on before they recover.'

Recover? What was she on about? And what had happened to her gag?

'What?' The word trickled from my mouth.

'Come on, Alice. Get a move on.'

I clambered from the floor and stumbled towards Cassie. She'd bitten through the gag, but that wasn't the most surprising sight. Rolling on the ground in spasms of shuddering jittering limbs were the angel and the demon, their faces contorted into parodies of humanity, which I guess is what they were.

I pulled at Cassie's ropes, breaking a nail as I got her free. 'What did you do to them?'

We stood together. As the angel thrashed around, his wings rippled against the floor. Cassie bent down and removed the knife from her jacket.

'I'm guessing it's what we did, maybe-sister, when they tried to consume us. We must be foul-tasting to their sensitive digestive systems.' She grinned with the whole of her face. 'Like extra-strong chilli or Marmite.'

The revelation punched me in the gut. 'We don't have human souls.'

'It would appear so. And it made them sick.' Cassie grabbed a handful of angel feathers.

'You aren't bothered?' I couldn't understand her casual attitude. The thought terrified me and I struggled to keep my trembling arms steady.

'It doesn't matter now. We'll find out what we are once we get what we want and travel back to our birth.'

She hacked at the wings. Agony consumed the angel's face, and I didn't know if it was because of what we'd done to him or because of Cassie slicing away at his back.

'We only need one feather. Why are you taking so many?'

She stood as she replied. 'You never know when they might come in handy. Do you want me to get the demon blood?'

'No. I'll do it.' I removed the syringe from my pocket and bent over the woman. Rage and agony filled her eyes, but she recognised what I was doing. I turned my head from her stare and took the blood.

'Time to go,' Cassie said as I stood.

Had we been out longer than thirty minutes? Would Kai abandon us if we had, and we'd have to leave this place the normal way and wander the streets of Los Angeles? We rushed down the stairs to discover our fate as an angel and demon howled upstairs.

20 TIME AFTER TIME

The gap was where we'd left it, a slice of reality flapping against the side as we approached. We went through and watched as Kai closed it behind us. She'd changed back into her male form, and it distracted me for a second. His beard had grown and he smelt of a dusky aftershave, even though he hadn't shaved. He said something to Cassie as I rushed to the bathroom, feet hitting the ground so hard, Rufus hurried out of my way. No sooner had I shut the door than I threw up in the sink. Bits of Bolognese and cheese floated around the bowl. The smell of it made me heave again. My throat throbbed, and my lungs quaked. Small creatures scuttled through my guts and I felt wretched.

'Are you okay, Alice?' Cassie banged on the door while the cat scratched at the bottom of the wood.

'I'm fine. I'll be out soon.' I turned on the tap and cleaned away the mess. I drank straight from the faucet, the cold water chilling my hands and throat. When I finished, I lifted my shirt and peered at the ribs the angel had broken. There was no scarring or bruises; no sign of what he'd done to me. I ran my fingers over my skin, trying to find how he'd healed me, but everything seemed normal.

But if I had no soul, how could I be normal?

I put my hand to my lips to stifle the laughter. There was me, the queen of logic and reason, believing in the soul. But why not? The supernatural was real, with angels and demons roaming the world, so why shouldn't humans have a soul, that divine connection to God?

I tried not to dwell on it, not to think if I was human or not, and checked my leg and foot. Everything was impossibly repaired. He'd said I'd be better than I was before. What did that mean? I appeared older in my reflection, bags under my eyes which I'm sure hadn't been there before we invaded Hollywood. I left the bathroom and returned to my bedroom for the Mirror and the Eye. The snake slumbered in the bag as I placed it inside my jacket.

As I re-joined them, Kai was rubbing his large hands together, staring at Cassie with wild eyes. 'You poisoned the angel and the demon?'

Cassie swigged from a bottle of Coke. 'It wasn't intentional, but I'm glad of the results. We'd have been dead otherwise.'

'We're not human?' I stared at the Warwitch. He shrugged.

'This is why you're going into the past and discovering the truth about yourselves.'

There was more than fascination in his face. Behind his large eyes, I detected something which hadn't been there before: fear.

I ignored that and asked the question bothering me the most. 'The soul is real?' Rufus followed me into the room and started purring against my leg. That was unusual.

Kai turned from my gaze as if it hurt his eyes. 'All

humans have souls. It's the Creator's grace passed on to those in his and her image.'

Cassie grabbed the cat and held him to her chest like a comfort blanket. 'So, those Celestials, the angel and the demon, feed on human souls like we eat caviar or the best steak.' She stared at me. 'Or whatever is at the top of the food chain for vegetarians.'

The Warwitch nodded. 'There is that, but also, some of them are jealous of what the Creator gave to humans, but not Celestials, so they want to drain it from you. The human soul is immortal, living on after the body has gone, so some Celestials believe devouring enough of them will extend their lives.'

A large part of my brain continued to consider the scientific reason for this, believing the human soul could be an energy field.

'Where does the soul come from? Are we born with it?'

Kai pursed his lips, looking more confused than enlightened. 'Every human religion and some supernatural ones mention souls and their importance, but no one knows where they are inside the body; only that they exist by the Grace of God.'

Cassie played with Rufus on the floor, tickling his belly and stroking his fur.

'And me and maybe-sister don't have them.'

'Perhaps you do, but the angel and demon had an allergic reaction to them.'

Cassie grinned at me as she pushed the can of pop to her mouth.

'We're the walking peanut girls.'

I didn't want to think about not having a soul. I didn't believe in souls, regardless of what the angel had bragged about. The snake moved around against my heart.

'It doesn't matter now.'

Cassie did her customary burp as she finished her drink and licked her lips.

'I thought angels were supposed to be the good guys?'

Kai walked to the end of the room and returned with a large dusty book. 'That's not always so. An angel is a supernatural being found in various religions and mythologies. Abrahamic religions often depict angels as benevolent celestial beings who act as intermediaries between God, or Heaven, and humanity. Other roles of angels include protecting and guiding humans and carrying out tasks on behalf of God. Abrahamic religions organise angels into hierarchies, although such rankings can vary between sects in each religion. Such angels may receive specific names, such as Gabriel or Michael, or titles such as seraph or archangel.'

I peered over his shoulder. 'Is that from the Bible?'

He had a glowing iPad between the pages of the book. 'No, it's from Wikipedia.'

Cassie joined us. 'I did a Google search for angels, and the first thing which came up was that terrible Robbie Williams tune. One of my foster carers was obsessed with the song, playing it repeatedly day after day. I nearly killed him for it.'

I stared at her, not knowing if she was joking or not. I turned back to Kai.

'Do you have any experience with angels?'

He narrowed his eyes and examined his nails. 'I try to avoid those at the very top of the supernatural tree. I've heard of their exploits and, to answer Cassie's original question, there are plenty of myths and legends about angels diverting from the Path of the Divine. The Creator wasn't happy with all of them.'

I put my hands to my chest, searching for broken bones and mystical pins holding me together.

'The angel crushed my ribs and broke my leg. He stamped on my foot, and it shattered.' My brain dragged the pain back as a jagged memory. 'I was dying; I know it. But then, I woke up healed again.' I didn't mention his claim of making me better than I was.

Kai took hold of my hands, concern in his face and warmth in his eyes. I'd thought the Warwitch's two genders differed in personality as well as body, but this kindness showed otherwise.

'From what I've learnt over the years, angels are difficult creatures to work out; their motivations always seem to be influenced by how the Creator treated them. Perhaps this one couldn't consume your soul if you're broken.'

Broken. For a long time, that's how I'd thought about myself: the broken child or the broken girl. But then, when I realised what was different about me was what made me special, I stopped thinking like that.

Yet, if Kai was right, maybe I'd been wrong all along.

I clasped the Mirror in my hand as the phone vibrated in my pocket. 'If those actors survive whatever we did to them, do you think they'll come after us for revenge?'

Kai shook his head. 'I don't believe angels or demons are creatures of vengeance. They have other desires to occupy them.'

The conversation bothered me. I wanted to forget about what had happened in LA and concentrate on what we had to do next.

'Are you sure this Mirror works as you claim?' I placed it on the table. 'When I used it on Medusa, all I saw was normal reflections.'

At the mention of her name, my phone pinged against

my leg again. I took it out and replied to her to let her know I was okay. She sent me a photograph of her head with a large red scarf covering the snakes. She wore sunglasses and had a massive grin on her face.

Kai picked up the Mirror. 'For the Mirror of Time to see into the past, the holder needs to focus on a specific point. You didn't do that on the island. Do you have the other objects?'

I held out the bag containing the Eye of Medusa and the vial of the demon blood. Cassie clutched a single angel feather.

Kai smiled where dark fuzz covered most of his face. 'Good. You both need to grasp the Mirror, focus on your birth, and then think of the name of the hospital.'

Cassie and I stared at each other and nodded.

I slipped the bag and vial into my jacket and did as Kai instructed, holding up the Mirror as our identical faces peered into the glass. It was unnerving to see myself like that, the reflection gazing back at me in stereo; only one half had part of an ear missing. In my head, I imaged being by the side of the bed after my mother had given birth, thinking of the name Saint Claire's.

But nothing happened.

'Are you concentrating, Alice?' Cassie said.

I wasn't. I couldn't think of the woman who gave me up. I thought of the alphabet and she wasn't there, with no letter X at the end.

And how could she be? I was the child of X, but I'd confined X to a past I didn't want to know anymore, an existence I didn't need.

'You must focus, Alice,' Cassie said.

So I dug deep into my mind, searching through those memories I'd confined to history, but which still lurked in the shadows. Ms Peel appeared first, with her glittering eyes and that smile that could warm the coldest winter days. She was the only woman I'd ever thought of as a substitute mother, and she was taken from me far too early.

I grasped the memory of my last meeting with her to my heart, but not my soul, and then delved into the earliest recollection I had, one I'd long forgotten until now. Female hands picked me up and carried me down a long corridor, while all around me, people shouted and screamed.

Then, inside the glass, our reflections disappeared, to be replaced by a swirl of dust or mist. My free hand drifted towards Cassie and we held on to each other. The mist vanished. The image in the Mirror was a long corridor dotted with signs on the wall. It was the corridor I'd just witnessed in my head. A man in a white uniform stepped into sight and walked down the passageway. My focus followed his walk to the end and the double doors saying Saint Claire's Hospital.

'That must be the place.'

'Good. Now you must use the Eye of Medusa to freeze that point before it loses shape and filters into another time, but make sure you don't gaze into the eyes of the snake. The Gorgon's curse can affect you even now.'

I let go of Cassie and the Mirror, removing the bag. I reached inside and grabbed the snake, which was once on the Gorgon's head. The creature didn't hiss or twist its body, its calm determined by my new friendship with Medusa. I removed the bag from the snake once I had it pointed towards the Mirror, expecting to freeze at its reflection, but it didn't appear there. When its eyes fell upon the glass, the image froze. I returned the snake to the bag, and then placed it on the table. Rufus jumped up and sniffed around it.

'Now it's a fixed point, so you can travel to it using the feather.' Kai's voice had risen a level, matching the excitement rippling through my veins.

Cassie held out the angel feather. 'How does this work?'

'Hold on to Alice with one hand, then place the feather on to the glass.'

Cassie looked at me, a signal travelling wordlessly between us. This was the last chance to change our minds, perhaps the final opportunity to walk away from all of this. There was a pause between us, and then I nodded at her.

'Before you go, remember to drink the demon blood when you step into the past. If you don't, you'll have no anchor there. You could drift away into any point in time and never be able to return here.'

The words startled me. 'We have to drink it? I thought we could hold it.'

Kai shook his head. 'You need it inside your bloodstream. Time is a living thing, and it will know you've invaded a point where you shouldn't be. It will try to reject you like antibodies attacking a virus.'

'How do we get back?' Cassie said.

'When you're ready, smash the Mirror.'

I gripped Cassie's fingers as she placed the angel feather on the glass. The temperature in the room increased, sweat dripping from my forehead. First, her hand disappeared, then her arm. Something dragged on her, hauling her into the Mirror in stages. It seemed as if she was shrinking by the second.

All I saw was the back of her head when she pulled me with her as if we were slipping underwater. I expected a psychedelic kaleidoscope when I stepped into the past, but it was like swimming through a door and into another room.

Only this door shimmered, and at the hinges, trembling shadows slipped out and drifted in front of me.

My body spun around, twisting and turning as a blazing white light covered my face. When my vision returned, I was the right way round, my balance returning to normal. My foot landed on the floor of the hospital when Cassie let go of me. I turned to see the Mirror of Time hanging in the air. It was suspended there for about thirty seconds before it dropped. I caught it before it hit the ground.

The feather had disappeared from Cassie's hand. 'Keep the Mirror close to you.' She stepped forward to read the directions on the wall. 'We need to find the maternity ward. Reception is through these doors.' The hospital had a strong smell of disinfectant seeping through it.

Cassie moved through the point where we'd seen the doctor go a few seconds earlier. I was following her, my legs like lead before an unseen force dragged me against the wall and up to the ceiling. Invisible hands clawed at my arms and legs as I slid against the cold concrete and towards the roof. Someone had placed a large weight on my stomach, my ribs appearing to shrink as I struggled to breathe. An antiseptic aroma rushed up my nose and dived into my throat. I wanted to gag.

'Alice!' Cassie yelled. Invisible fingers pressed a hammer against my heart. My hands vibrated on a different frequency, turning translucent in front of my eyes. 'Drink the demon blood, Alice.' As she shouted, something ripped Cassie from the floor and into the wall opposite me.

I felt my body slipping away as time rejected us. We crawled up opposite walls against our will, with unseen hands pushing me towards the ceiling. My lungs and chest shrivelled towards each other as I reached into my pocket.

Across from me, Cassie's cheeks rippled like water, and the gravity of time began to push her nose apart.

Energy trickled through me from somewhere and I removed the phial from my pocket. It shook in my fingers, slithering from them and floating away. I watched it drop to the ground in slow motion as I heard Cassie's anguished cry crawl from her mouth and linger in the air.

Then my other hand thrust forward and I caught it. I tore off the top and drank half of the blood in one go.

The effects were immediate as I slipped down the wall and hit the ground. I jumped upwards and looked at Cassie. Her body was fading into nothing. One hand reached down to me and I threw the phial to her, gazing in agony as she clutched at it. She caught the end of the glass as her fingers trembled. She pushed it to her mouth and drained the phial. It was a long drop from the ceiling, but I grabbed her as she fell. We ended up in a heap on the cold ground, arms around each other. The weight of the universe had left me, and now I was light enough to float away again.

She pulled up and wiped red from her lips. 'I thought it would taste worse than that.'

I rolled from her. 'It was sweet, like honey.'

'What are you girls doing down there?' The doctor from earlier had returned.

I found energy from somewhere and jumped to my feet. 'Can you point us in the direction of the maternity ward, please?'

When he did, we were off and running towards the lift and the third floor.

'I went from feeling crap to feeling great,' Cassie said as she pushed a button.

'Do you think we're in the past?' I said as the door closed and we headed up.

'I guess we'll find out soon enough. Just don't lose that Mirror, sister.'

It was the first time she'd called me that and my heart skipped a beat. The lift opened, and we stumbled into bright whiteness and the smell of surgical cleanliness.

'Can I help you, girls?' A nurse with a stern smile stood between us and everywhere else.

For some reason, Cassie adopted an accent of broken English.

'We're looking fer ur aunty. She's just ad twin gurls.'

'What's her name?' She glared at Cassie as my maybe-probably-sister struggled with a reply. We didn't have a name apart from the ones we had been given in our respective orphanages: Valentine for me, Kane for her. Would it be one of those?

'Oh wait; I can see the resemblance to your aunt in your eyes. You must be looking for Mary Arcane. She's in the last room on your left at the end of this corridor.' And with that, she went before we could thank her.

We had a name for our mother. And one for us.

Arcane. Mary Arcane.

The sisters Arcane.

Cassie grabbed my hand. I was getting used to the warmth human contact provided and didn't want to let go. I didn't want her to let go.

'Do you think Arcane is our real name? Cassie and Alice Arcane sounds cool.'

For the first time since we'd met, Cassie resembled the teenager she was.

I pulled her in front of me as we hurried towards the room.

'Let's ask her and find out.'

We sprinted down the empty corridor, my brain banging against the insides of my skull, one hand clinging on to Cassie's fingers. Then my other hand was on the door. Every organ in my body vibrated at a different frequency, my heart fit to burst.

I hesitated. Cassie pushed me inside.

I'd been in hospital rooms before. Once, when a grumpy doctor removed my tonsils because they'd turned black and poisonous; another time when I'd knelt on a piece of glass and it went straight through the flesh below my knee. I still had the scar for that. This room did not differ from those others: clean, spotlessly white and smelling of antiseptic and fresh flowers. There were roses near the bed. The bed my mother lay in. Was this my mother? Was this our mother?

'Mary?' Cassie let go of me and moved forward. My legs froze to the spot. Would I dare ask this woman why she'd given me away, why she'd abandoned us?

Cassie turned to me. 'Come here, Alice.'

I retook her hand and approached the bed. I peered into

an older version of myself. Apart from the long snow-white hair resting on her shoulders, she was the spitting image of Cassie and me. And she was in a deep, deep sleep.

'Hello, Mother X.' My voice sounded squeaky and tinny to my ears. All those times I'd stared at the letter X next to my name or the redacted name of the woman who'd given me away, I'd never expected to be in this moment. Not the moment of travelling back in time and standing at her bed, but of coming face to face with her. The fact she was asleep made it easier for me. If she'd been awake, what would I have said to her? Why did you throw me away? Why did you separate me from my twin sister? Would my life have been better if any of us had stayed together from this point? Would I still have been as lonely?

'I guess squeezing us from her belly took a lot from her.' Cassie's flippancy startled me until I realised it was to cover her nerves. Lines of anxiety hid below her lips, trembling on her skin. We stood in silence and gazed at our mother. She looked so peaceful. I held her hand in mine and felt the connection between us. I would have described her as angelic if not for my recent experience with that cruel and capricious heavenly creature.

'Should we wake her up?' The idea both excited and terrified me. I could tell her I'd battled supernatural creatures and broken the laws of physics to find out why she'd given me away, or perhaps I'd talk about my academic achievements and my entry into university at sixteen.

'She's heavily sedated until we move her somewhere safer.'

The voice shook me from my reverie. I let go of Cassie and Mary and turned to see the newcomer in the room. Her black hair was tied tightly on her head, its darkness contrasting with the whiteness of the coat she wore. Stick-like legs stuck out from the bottom, so thin I thought they'd snap if she moved. Her eyes blazed like lights in the night sky. Fixed to her chest was a label with the name Lucy Star handwritten on it.

My hands trembled and I didn't know why. There was something about her, something which made me uneasy. In one of my many foster homes, before Artemis rescued me, I'd been forced to take therapy sessions from a woman who appeared responsible and knowledgeable, but who turned out to enjoy the suffering of others. This woman in the hospital room reminded me of her.

Cassie stepped away from me. 'Are you her doctor?'

The woman, who I assumed was Lucy, pouted and rolled her eyes. She removed a lipstick from her pocket and applied it before she spoke, a vibrant purple colour which smelt of Palma Violets. It glistened as she parted her mouth.

'I've gazed and peered over numerous bodies, far too many to count, sliced and diced until there was nothing but red in front of me. I'm infectious and sometimes a panacea for what ails you. But I'm not a doctor.'

I moved next to Cassie, scrutinising this strange woman. 'Who are you?'

She ripped the label from her coat and threw it at me; it bounced off my chest and fell to the floor.

'I'm Lucy. And you're Alice, and that's Cassandra. You know, I never would have found you again if you hadn't travelled here. Your mother's energy prevents any Celestial from travelling through time to her, but once you two opened the door, I knew it was there and stepped through it.' She glanced around the room. 'You drank some demon blood to keep you here, which is impressive, but if I heard the door opening, then so will others. I won't be the only one coming here, so you two better get a move on and come with me. There's nothing you can do for your mother, and the babies have been moved from the building, as I already know to my great distress.' She examined us like a scientist studying bugs under a magnifying glass.

'We're not going anywhere with you.' Cassie had her blade out. I was too slow again, but it wouldn't have mattered this time. With one wave of Lucy's hand, we were thrown backwards and pinned against the wall. A river of pain flowed down my spine as I struggled against an immovable invisible force. Cassie's face rippled from the pressure. The woman ignored my shout of frustration and sat in the chair opposite the bed. She removed a Vape stick from her white coat. She sucked on it and blew out a sickly sweet smell of cranberries.

'I hate these things.' She sucked on it again. 'The only reason I travel back in time nowadays is to have a cigarette with a pint in a pub.' She waved the Vape in the air. 'This is not progress.'

'Let us go and you can smoke on my fist.' Cassie's defiance gave me strength. My fingers were free of the wall.

'Your mother did well to hide you for so long, but it would always end up like this.' An orange-tinted vapour drifted from her mouth. 'A younger version of me is scouring the hospital as I speak, searching for you two as babies. It was tempting to wait here for that version of me to tell her not to waste sixteen years searching for you both, but I wasn't a pleasant person then, so best to be avoided. She can pack your mother off, and I'll have you two now.'

As she finished speaking, a flutter of wings echoed around the room, to be followed by the entrance of the most handsome man I'd ever seen, even better looking than Dracula. His was a presence that stopped you dead in your tracks: tall, slim, muscular, with an almost perfectly symmetrical face.

Lucy curled her lips at him. 'I thought you'd have been here sooner, Michael.'

'I was too busy cleaning up another of your messes in North America, Sibling.' Michael turned those magnetic eyes on Cassie, and then me. 'So, these are the Arcane twins who escaped our grasp on this day of their birth?' He grinned and the temperature of the room increased, my clothes sticking to me as if I was at the hottest gig ever, and a thousand people squashed me against this wall. His smile was so wide, it was as if he wanted to eat us. 'And now they're all grown up, which is perfect.'

Lucy blew flavoured smoke in his direction. 'So, what now, Brother? Are we to fight over these strays, bring down this building and everyone in it, including our younger selves?'

Michael pressed his hands together and contemplated her question. 'I hate bumping into other versions of me; the conversation is always so dull.'

'So, what do you suggest, Brother?'

'Dear Sister, since you're always so keen to do deals, why not let the girls choose who they'll leave with? It will save so much time and destruction.'

'We're not going anywhere with either of you,' Cassie snarled as she struggled against her restraints. Both my hands and legs were free, though I didn't move them. It was only my back I needed to release. Maybe the Hollywood angel had given me increased strength when he'd healed the body he broke.

Michael floated from the floor and crossed his legs. 'You girls need to understand something about your history before you make any rash decisions.' He drifted over the bed and peered at Mary Arcane. Then he returned his gaze to us. 'You don't know what you are, do you?' He seemed amused by the thought.

'Is it wise to tell them, Brother?' Lucy dropped her Vape to the floor, where it rattled and rolled under my feet. Her breathing was shallow, appearing to be caught in her lungs as she spoke.

'How could any girl resist a plan so devious?' Michael looked down at the woman he called Sister. 'How can they be part of the solution if they don't know their history?'

I didn't care what they were talking about or their stupid plans, hoping they'd be distracted enough for me to pull away from the wall. What I'd do then was another thing altogether. But at least I'd remembered what Kai had said back in the Impossible Palace about angels and heavenly hierarchies; these two were archangels. They ignored us and stared at each other. Then Michael tore his gaze from Lucy and peered into my face.

'Your mother is the last of the Nephilim. Do you know what they are, child?'

This ancient creature was so lost in his arrogance that he felt nothing for Cassie and me. I answered his question, a vague recollection of the name floating around inside my brain.

'Aren't they mentioned in the Bible?'

'Yes, child; well done.' Michael hovered over my mother and continued to educate us. 'The Nephilim were the offspring of humans and angels.' His face sparkled as he spoke. 'God the Almighty, the Creator of all living things, forbade angels from having personal relationships, so some of my brethren, in their frustration, cast their eyes over humanity. God forbade relationships between angels and humans, but a few ignored this and sired children with humans. These children were the Nephilim, the sight of whom angered God to a fury.'

Anger burnt through Michael's orbs, which turned red and shimmered.

'To remove this unholy spawn from the planet, God the Almighty sent a great flood to wipe the Earth clean, only saving a few of their creations. It was believed the Nephilim were destroyed when the waters consumed the world, but this wasn't so. And now we have you two, the Children of the Nephilim.'

Is this why Kai couldn't see into us, why we have no souls, and why our blood poisoned the angel and the demon? As these questions pounded my brain, I pulled away from the wall, the force which had kept me there gone. But I didn't fall. I was floating and couldn't understand how.

Michael moved the hair from my mother's face and I wanted to strangle him. I resisted the urge and clung to the wall.

'Brother, will you not tell them the whole truth so they can choose a side?' Lucy grinned as Michael grimaced. The handsome archangel turned back to me.

'God the Almighty abandoned their creations over two millennia ago, saddened at what had become of their human children.' Sorrow seeped from him like a cascading waterfall. 'But the Creator is returning to wipe the Earth clean once more and to start all over again. My dear sibling, Lucy Morningstar, has promised to stop this and is busy gathering an army to her side to oppose the Creator. The angels will not allow this to happen. It's our job to prepare the way for the cleansing to come.'

'What have we got to do with this?' Cassie said.

'There is a prophecy that the Children of the Nephilim are weapons of mass destruction, the only creatures capable of defeating God the Almighty, which means you have to choose a side now.'

Cassie still struggled under Lucy's influence as I watched her try to pull from the wall. Whatever I had done was impossible for her.

'And what if we want nothing to do with either of you?'

'That is not a choice. If you refuse me, I'll have no option but to kill you both.' Michael floated between Cassie and me. 'Your true power is beyond you without guidance and training. If you don't take my offer, I'll snuff out your potential like a candle.'

'Girls, how can you trust a man who speaks to you like that?' Lucy laughed, and in that instant, I threw myself at Michael. I hit him full-on, tearing him away from Cassie and across the room, where the force sent us back and into Lucy in her seat. All three of us hit the floor together. The crash behind me had to be Cassie falling after my attack removed Lucy's influence.

I jumped up and turned to her.

'Come on,' I shouted as I ran to the door. I burst through it, lungs beating like an asthmatic butterfly. I turned to see Cassie as an enormous explosion of light burst from my mother's room and blew my sister and me into the corridor.

We hit the wall together, pain shooting down my side as we rolled across the floor. I staggered up first and pulled Cassie with me. The light coming out of the room was so bright, I had to shield my eyes. And the noise was so loud, I couldn't hear what Cassie said to me.

'What?' I said as she pulled me to the side.

'What do we do now? We can't leave our mother with them.'

Before I could reply, the archangel Michael burst through the door and hit the same wall we'd just done.

Bright light shimmered around him as the heat forced Cassie and me back. I didn't know what was happening, but it had to be worse than dealing with an angel and a demon.

'We have to leave,' I shouted as the floor outside my mother's room vibrated and moved like hot concrete.

Cassie grabbed me. 'We can't leave her with them.'

A howling shriek burst from the room as the light disappeared from Michael and he glared at me. Ice-cold fingers grabbed at my heart and I was ready to fall into the abyss. His eyes were dark pits as he got up and reached for me.

Then Cassie pulled me away and we were running down the corridor. Behind us came an unearthly howl as heat burnt at my neck. The Mirror of Time was in my hand as we ran. I threw it to the ground, the glass shattering in front of me.

This time, there was a tornado of activity everywhere and, as I spun with my hand outstretched, Cassie grabbed hold of me. Dust and air swirled around us as gravity or something else pushed us forward. Blue streams of electricity shimmered in the air. Something moved me on until I stopped. I turned to look at Cassie, but near her, reaching out for her leg, was a horror beyond my imagination. The reddest of ruby eyes glared at me, containing all the evil and hate in the world. The air stank of sulphur and brimstone, with my ears assaulted by the screams of every dead thing walking the Earth. Fingers longer than skyscrapers crept towards Cassie. Yellowed nails clutched at her skin as a blackened tongue shot from that reddened skull and struck at her waist. We were about to be pulled back when we hit the floor in the Impossible Palace.

My breathing returned to normal as I stared at the ceiling. I turned to Cassie as the Mirror of Time dropped out of the air and landed on my chest.

'Remind me never to do that again,' Cassie said.

And then we laughed, a great release of terror and anxiety. I lay on my back, holding her hand, and wondered if I'd ever return to university. How could science explain any of this?

'So, did you find what you wanted?' Kai, now returned to her female form, gazed at us. We stayed there for an indeterminate time before telling our story.

It was the story of the Children of the Nephilim.

Kai leant back into the chair, Rufus circling at her feet.

'You're the Children of the Nephilim?' She stared at us with a mixture of admiration, fear and curiosity. I didn't blame her. I felt the same way. 'The offspring of the "sons of God" and the "daughters of men" have led to you? This explains why I cannot see your past or future. And why the angel and demon tasted poison when they tried to consume your souls.'

Cassie rubbed at her damaged ear. 'So our mother, Mary Arcane, who we saw in that hospital bed, isn't human?'

I couldn't tell if she was pleased or disgusted by the thought. Hunting and killing monsters had consumed her life for so long, but now she and I were likely as inhuman as the things she'd killed.

Kai stood and reached for a bottle of dark liquid near her. There was a slight tremor in her fingers, and she poured herself a drink without offering us one. She raised the glass to her lips and lowered her eyes to us.

'If it's true what the archangels told you, and we've no guarantee they weren't lying, then your mother as a Nephilim would be the offspring of an angel and human woman. So she's half-human, and you two are half that again.'

'It doesn't explain why those archangels would fight over us,' Cassie said.

It was something I'd been deliberating over since we'd returned to the present. 'They said we're the Children of the Nephilim. What if that means it wasn't only mother who was a Nephilim, but our father as well?'

Kai's jaw dropped at my question. 'There was no sight or mention of your father in the hospital?'

I shook my head. 'Everything went by in a blur. We'd barely got to the room when Lucy and Michael appeared.'

Cassie polished her ear so much, I thought it would disappear. 'Let's assume that was our mother and we are these Children of the Nephilim.' She glanced at me. 'Why are we so important to them?'

'We're important to stop something terrible happening to the world,' I said.

'You mean God returning to wipe the planet clean?' Kai's voice trembled when she spoke, her fingers tapping on her leg.

'Yeah; how can Alice and I stop such a thing?'

'Because you're the purest form of God's essence.' Kai ran a finger across her top lip. 'You have the blood of a Celestial with the soul of humanity.'

'But I thought we didn't have souls,' I said. 'Isn't that why the demon and angel became ill once they tried to drink ours? And why you can't see into our lives?'

Kai put the glass to one side, still with that slight tremble in her fingers.

'I'm guessing what you have aren't souls as humans have them, but something changed, perhaps even enhanced.'

'So you think we have souls, but they're different from other humans because of our parents, or at least our mother?' I wasn't the child of X, but something beyond the alphabet.

Kai's fingers stopped shaking and she placed them on her heart.

'It seems the likeliest explanation from what sounds unexplainable. And there are two of you. You must be unique in both worlds, of humanity and the supernatural. If the archangels presume you to be beings of great potential, that knowledge probably leaked out to other Celestials. This would explain why someone put a contract out on Cassie, and why Michael and Lucy wanted to abduct you.'

Cassie moved closer to me. 'But you didn't know who we are when we first arrived, yet you gave us the impression you know everything that happens in Whitby regarding supernatural creatures and events.'

Rufus continued to rub against Kai's leg. 'That is strange.' She peered straight at me. 'I sensed your energy as soon as you entered the town, and it only grew stronger the closer you got to me. But I couldn't recognise you as the offspring of the Nephilim because I have no reference for that. The Nephilim were supposedly wiped out centuries ago.'

I stared at Kai, seeing her, but not seeing her, still wondering if she'd sent us for the artefacts for herself and not to help us. Yet, even after Dr Rivers had betrayed us at the Nexus, I still wanted to trust her.

'If Michael and Lucy have searched for Cassie and me for sixteen years, perhaps they've somehow kept our existence secret from people like you, Kai.'

'What's so special about them?' Cassie's lack of Biblical knowledge surprised me. Most of the foster homes I'd lived in were religious, where sermons and people preaching at the kids were a regular occurrence. I'd always wondered if having to listen to that every day had turned me into an atheist. And a lot of good that did me since I now appeared to have proof that angels and demons exist, and probably a God who created them and everything else.

I dug deep into my memory and remembered a particular Sunday of church education.

'In the New Testament, Michael leads God's armies against Satan's forces in the Book of Revelation, where he defeats Satan during the war in Heaven.'

Cassie ran her fingers through her hair, tugging at the ends.

'This is Satan as in Lucifer, as in Lucy?'

I made a fake movement of slapping my hand up to my forehead.

'Lucy Morningstar. I should have realised it as soon as they started that weird conversation.'

'So Satan is a woman now?'

Kai dropped a tattered book on to the table, the dust jumping off it and swirling in the air.

'This version of the Old Testament is based on the Tanakh, the Hebrew Bible.' She opened it, flicking through the pages as if speed reading. 'In it is the oldest mention of Satan. In Hebrew, the translation of the term "Satan" is usually "opponent" or "adversary". It is often understood to represent the sinful impulse or the forces which prevent human beings from submitting to divine will.'

Cassie snorted through her nose. 'That sounds like a man to me.'

Kai continued, 'Lucifer, the "light-bringer", is the Latin

name for the planet Venus as the morning star in the ancient Roman era, and is often used for mythological and religious figures associated with the planet.'

I scratched my head. 'And Venus is the Roman goddess of love.'

'This is hurting my brain,' Cassie said.

I picked up the Mirror of Time and peered into it, imagining an older version of myself. 'I don't care about any of this: Lucifer or Lucy, God and archangels, of Heaven and Hell. All I want is to rescue our mother from wherever Lucy took her.'

Cassie nodded at me. 'Alice is right. It doesn't matter who they claim to be or whether that nonsense about God returning here to rid the world of humans is true or not. We only did this to discover why our mother gave us away sixteen years ago, and now we know she didn't do that.' She put her hand on my arm. 'We were taken from her, and all I care about is finding her again. Michael and Lucy, or whoever she is, can do whatever they want with the world as long as we find our mother.'

I nodded and put my hand in hers: my sister. 'Perhaps we should use the Mirror to return to the hospital and see what happened to her?'

Cassie clenched her jaw, the sound of her grinding teeth making Rufus jump.

'I think it would be too risky, Alice. We don't know what would happen if we bumped into the other versions of ourselves, and Michael and Lucy might still be there. And we drank all the demon blood. We need to find Mother now, in the present.' She didn't mention having a stack full of angel feathers hidden away somewhere.

I put the Mirror down, glad not to go through the time-travelling experience again. Kai glanced from me to the Mirror before picking the cat up.

'Travelling through time should always be a last resort.' Rufus purred in her hands. 'And remember what you told me about Lucy sensing you'd gone back in time, and that's how she found you at the hospital. It might be better if you left the Mirror and the Eye of Medusa with me for safe-keeping.'

Did Kai know about Lucy all along; that once we opened the portal into the past, the archangels would know where we were? I retrieved the Mirror and slipped it into my pocket.

'No, we could still use these to find our mother because I can think of only one place Lucy would have taken her sixteen years ago.'

Cassie grinned at me. 'You're right.' She slapped her hands together. 'People have been telling me I'd go to Hell all my life, and it looks like they were spot on.'

Kai pulled at Rufus's hair and the cat twitched in her hands. 'You want to go to Hell? Do you think that's wise after what happened with Lucy at the hospital?'

I ignored her concerns. 'Will the Blade of Reality cut us a doorway into Hell?' I'd lost all sense of reason and logic as the science in my brain shrank into the darkness. Angels existed, the First of the Fallen was real, and a woman, so Heaven and Hell must be somewhere.

Kai screwed up her face. 'No. Even if Hell were on Earth, I'd need to know where it is, to see it in my mind to slice a way through to it. That's how the Blade of Reality works.'

Cassie bit her lip. 'That's a stupid name for the knife. It should be called the Blade of Geography.'

A plan formed inside my head. 'Let's assume Heaven

and Hell are real and they're not places on Earth, which means they must exist in some other reality, like a separate dimension from ours. I think the Blade could cut us into Hell, but we haven't got time to work it out. We have to find another way to get there.' They both looked at me. 'Since demons populate Hell, we have to ask one of them how to do it.'

Cassie jumped up. 'Let's return to Hollywood and interrogate that stupid actress.'

'It's tempting, but too dangerous.' There was no way I wanted a return meeting with the angel who'd broken me and put me back together. 'We need a different demon.' I hadn't worked that part out yet.

I stood with Cassie, my mind focused on the quest to find our mother, and my head filled with images of her in that hospital bed. Had she given me away not because she didn't want me, not because she felt nothing for me, not to separate me from Cassie, but to protect us both?

Kai dropped Rufus to the carpet and placed her hands on our shoulders. 'You needn't go far.'

'What do you mean?' Cassie and I spoke in stereo.

'There is a demon tethered to this abbey.'

'Just when I thought nothing else could surprise me,' I said.

The Warwitch removed her hands from us. 'When the world was more religious than it is now, demons would gravitate to every recognised place of worship. The souls of the devout are much sweeter to consume for them. Captured demons were imprisoned and tethered to the property as warnings for others to keep away or suffer the same fate, which is why there's still one here. Shall I take you to it?'

'What a stupid question.' I was up and dragging Cassie

from the room, fingers trembling with excitement. 'Where is it?'

Kai stumbled behind me. 'Wait, Alice, wait. I need to get something first.'

I let go of Cassie as Kai ducked into the next room. There was a lot of banging and cursing before she reappeared, carrying a dusty wooden box. She placed it on the table and grinned at me.

'What's inside there?' I said.

She opened it and reached inside.

Then she pulled out the pistol and pointed it straight between my eyes.

I stared at Kai, the Warwitch of Whitby, as she pointed the pistol at my face. At my side was my sister, Cassie, seemingly ready to pounce on the guardian of the Impossible Palace and save me from certain death.

Then Kai grinned and put down the gun. 'That's Blackbeard's cutlass, but it's his glove we need.' She reached into the box and took out a glove. 'We need this to access the demon. Its name is Bartos.'

Cassie narrowed her eyes. 'For one second, I thought you were going to shoot my sister, Kai.'

The Warwitch laughed. 'Now, why would I do that, Cassandra Arcane?'

I clutched at my chest to calm my beating heart. 'This demon will show us how to enter Hell?'

Kai nodded. 'Are you both ready?'

I looked at Cassie, an unspoken message travelling between us.

Now we'd search for our mother.

After we went Hell.

THANK YOU!

Thank you, dear reader for purchasing this book.

If you enjoyed reading about Alice and Cassie Arcane their journey continues in these books:

The Arcane Supernatural Thriller Series
Book one: The Arcane
Book two: The Arcane Identity
Book three: The Arcane Quest
Book four: The Arcane Ultimatum

Many thanks to my wonderful wife for all her support and patience.

My eternal gratitude to Wendy Cross for being the first person to read the Arcane and who gave me essential feedback on the characters and the plot.

Extra special thanks to Karina Gallagher for being a dedicated reader of my work.

The Arcane edited by Alison Jack.

Cover design by James, GoOnWrite.com

Andrew French lives amongst faded seaside glamour on the North East coast of England. He likes gin and cats but not together, new music and old movies, curry and ice cream. Slow bike rides and long walks to the pub are his usual exercise, as well as flicking through the pages of good books and the memoirs of bad people.

Find out more at www.andrewsfrench.com

Facebook:

https://www.facebook.com/A-S-French-Author-150145625006018

Twitter:

www.twitter.com/andrewfrench100

Instagram:

www.instagram.com/andrewfrench100

And replies to all his email at mail@andrewsfrench.com

If you have the time, please leave a review at Amazon or Goodreads

Thank you!